BRING OUT THE THE BANNERS

GEOFFREY TREASE

WALKER BOOKS
AND SUBSIDIARIES
LONDON · BOSTON · SYDNEY

First published 1994 by Walker Books Ltd
87 Vauxhall Walk, London SE11 5HJ

This edition published 1995

2 4 6 8 10 9 7 5 3 1

Text © 1994 Geoffrey Trease
Cover illustration © 1994 Anne Yvonne Gilbert

The right of Geoffrey Trease to be identified as
author of this work has been asserted by
him in accordance with the Copyrights,
Designs and Patents Act 1988.

This book has been typeset in Sabon.

Printed in Great Britain

British Library Cataloguing in Publication Data
A catalogue record for this book is
available from the British Library.

ISBN 0-7445-3618-9

For Linda and Mike and Sophie

CHAPTER ONE

The young man intrigued her from the moment he slipped aboard, just as the bearded fisherman was casting off. In his town overcoat and hat he could scarcely be one of the crew.

He stood close to her as they chugged away from the quay. "Will it be rough?" she asked.

"Bit choppy, maybe, in the outer harbour." He did not speak like a Plymouth man. "You're not worried?"

"Oh, no, I'm a good sailor." She could only hope she was. She could not afford to be queasy today. She had been brought on this adventure only because no one else knew shorthand. It could be vital to have an exact record of anything said. A thrilling responsibility.

The young man made no effort to continue the conversation. He seemed preoccupied, glancing round at the older women with an observant look.

Mrs Blake beckoned her aft.

"Who is *he*, Fiona?"

"I've no idea, Mrs Blake. I supposed he had something to do with the boat – "

"So did I. But the skipper thought he was with us."

Fiona turned to look back at the stranger. His manner had impressed her, but she guessed now that he was hardly older than herself. "With *us*?" she echoed in surprise. There were of course no men in their little party from London. The Women's Social and Political Union welcomed male sympathizers but they could not become members, much less join in a secret mission like today's. "He seems quite harmless," she said.

"We can hardly throw him overboard now," said Mrs Blake humorously.

Fiona had no desire to do so. She said, with an answering laugh, "And we *are* supposed to be non-violent!"

They moved forward into the bows, Mrs Blake clutching at her hat as they met the force of the wind. Even her long hatpins were hardly enough to keep it on. Fiona pulled up her hood, the spray cold on her cheeks as the little craft cut through the water.

On this leaden December morning in 1913 Plymouth Sound looked grey and unromantic. No other small vessels were in sight. There were two warships at their moorings, like spectral sea-monsters. Further out lay their objective, the White Star liner *Majestic* from New York, anchored according to custom two miles out, waiting for the tender.

"We must put on our sashes," said Mrs Blake.

They took them out and slung them over their right shoulders. The boldly-lettered slogan, VOTES FOR WOMEN, spoke for all who claimed the suffrage, the equal right with men to choose the nation's government, but the distinctive purple, green and white colours of the W.S.P.U. identified them as militants, determined on action. It was the *Daily Mail* that had first dubbed them "Suffragettes" but they had adopted the nickname with pride.

"The skipper will go as close as he can and circle the ship. She's sure to be on deck. You've a good strong voice, my dear. It should carry."

Fiona grinned. "My brothers complain!"

"And what do we shout?"

"'The cats are here, Mrs Pankhurst, they're close on you!'"

Mrs Blake nodded approvingly. "'But we're here to take you off!'"

"Do you think the captain will let us?"

"Mrs Pankhurst is a very determined lady. She is a British citizen, she has a right to enter her own country."

It should be quite simple. The liner had only to let down a gangway and she could step straight into their boat.

Years later, looking back, Fiona would marvel at Mrs Blake's confidence. But of course, it had been 1913, in a vanished age. In 1913, if you were

British, you could travel through most of the world without even a passport.

Now, as the motorboat surged forward, she rehearsed the words once more in her head. "'The cats are here, Mrs Pankhurst – '" Her lips were dry with nervousness.

The police had won their nickname with the notorious Cat-and-Mouse Act. If a suffragette went on hunger-strike in prison she was released before she could die, for it would never do for a woman to die while a prisoner. As soon as she was sufficiently recovered the police pounced and she was taken back to continue her sentence. Mrs Pankhurst was the most famous mouse of all. Nothing would break her determination to win the vote for women. She had been in and out of prison four times this year. Today, when she returned from her speaking tour in America, the police planned to arrest her again.

It was to prevent this that Fiona's party had come down from London.

She turned her head, ducking the wind, and glanced back at the young stranger. He looked even younger now, hatless, his hair flicking about his temples.

She caught the peal of his laughter as he joked with the fishermen. Unreasonably she resented their laughter. This was not the moment. But of course – men! Some were imaginative enough to sympathize. Most thought the suffragette campaign was just funny.

She blinked into the wind again with narrowed eyes. The liner loomed ahead, a cliff of sheer steel against the sky.

CHAPTER TWO

On deck, an hour earlier, another girl had been similarly nerving herself – but only to speak to the fellow passenger beside her, leaning on the rail.

This was her last chance. Soon they would be docking, streaming down gangways in a flurry of farewells, finding seats in the boat train for London. The opportunity to speak to the notorious Mrs Pankhurst would have gone.

Throughout the Atlantic crossing Belle had been studying her from afar. On the first evening the news had spread through the ship that Emmeline Pankhurst was on board. Belle had quickly identified her from her newspaper photographs. Half the passengers were eager to talk to this formidable lady. The other half wanted only the chance to ignore her pointedly and sweep grandly by, staring through her as if she were no more than a plain glass window, and a rather dirty one at that. A little crowd was usually gathered round her.

Now, at close quarters, Belle was more than ever impressed by her slender elegance. She did not look like an agitator who swayed immense audiences. But, as Belle had heard, she had been sent to Paris at fifteen to finish her education, and that spell in the French capital had given her a poise and a dress sense that she had never lost in the later years of widowhood, financial difficulty and campaigning for the cause she believed in.

Belle moistened her lips. She must speak, if only the most ordinary remark. "We shall be home in good time for Christmas," she said.

Mrs Pankhurst swung round and smiled. "Yes. Though I am not quite sure," she added with irony, "where I shall be spending the festive season."

"I wish I could have heard your speech in New York! But Mother and I were visiting friends in Boston. You had a tremendous welcome!"

"The American public is sympathetic to the suffrage movement." Mrs Pankhurst smiled again. "You clearly know who *I* am. May I know..."

"Oh, I'm sorry. My name's Isherwood. My friends call me 'Belle'."

"And others, I imagine, call you 'Lady Isabel'?"

"Actually – yes." Belle flushed, surprised by this quick identification.

"And your father is the Earl of Cleveland?"

"Yes."

"One of the more enlightened men in the House

13

of Lords, if I may say so! I saw your mother's name on the passenger list. I was sorry he was not with you. Tell me, my dear, how long have you been interested in the suffrage question?"

"Only since last summer. Derby Day, actually."

"Ah, *Derby* Day." Mrs Pankhurst's tone was heavy with meaning. "Odd that a horse race should set so many people thinking about votes or women."

Belle's memories came flashing back. The December morning became an afternoon in June. She and her brother had left their parents in the stand. More exciting, said Edward, to mix with the crowd. He placed a bet for her with a huge red-faced bookmaker in a loud-checked suit. Patriotically she backed the King's horse, Anmer. They pushed their way to the rails at Tattenham Corner, to get a good view of the horses coming round the final bend.

"Here they come!" cried Edward, shaken for once out of his languid Cambridge manner.

The drumming of hoofs was deafening, the horses mere streaks of speed, the jockeys crouching manikins.

"He's left it too late," Edward exclaimed in disgust. "Anmer will never make it now – " His tone changed suddenly. "Dam' fool of a woman! What does she think..." His words were lost in the roar of shock and horror from the crowd.

Belle could see it all still, six months later, photographed on her mind's eye like moving pictures.

14

The King's horse turning a somersault, the jockey flying through the air… She loved horses and her first thought was for Anmer. To her immense relief the horse was struggling to its feet, apparently unhurt. The jockey too was standing up, seizing the bridle, stroking the glossy neck.

Only the dark figure of the woman on the ground was motionless. Ambulance men were racing across to her.

The crowd was in tumult. Edward had lost the last trace of his university languor. "Serve her right! Running out like that – bloody suffragette!"

It had seemed absurd afterwards – amid all that horror to feel an instinctive shock at her brother swearing in a public place. He ignored her scandalized gasp. "You've left school," he reminded her afterwards. "I bet King George was saying worse. *His* horse! They say he can cuss like a sailor!"

From these memories Belle was brought back to the present by Mrs Pankhurst's quiet voice.

"Poor Miss Davison! She never told anyone beforehand. We'd never have approved of anything so dangerous." Edward, Belle recalled, had dismissed the dead woman as a crazy crank. But Mrs Pankhurst continued: "Such a brilliant woman! First-class honours at Oxford – they let women take the exams, but they can't have the degree!"

"It's so *unfair*!"

"London University is more modern. Emily

took her BA there. There was nothing wrong with her brain."

At this point she was interrupted by a ship's boy, almost bursting with excitement. "Beg pardon, madam – the purser's compliments, and would you be good enough to come below to his office?"

"I've been expecting this," murmured Mrs Pankhurst. "A marvellous invention, this wireless." She fixed the boy with a magnetic eye. "My compliments to the purser – but I shall do nothing of the kind."

Everything happened then with lightning speed. There was a rush of heavy booted feet across the deck. Belle was pushed roughly aside, Mrs Pankhurst disappeared into a little group of figures and was hustled protesting away.

A crowd of passengers gathered like magic. There was a concerted rush to the rails on the other side. Fighting her way there, Belle craned over and saw a lowered gangway slanting down to a broad-beamed tug that was bobbing on the water alongside. She was in time to see Mrs Pankhurst being dragged down and lifted aboard.

"Cor, there's enough of 'em!" said a deck hand beside her. "Five Scotland Yard men, two from the Plymouth police and a wardress from Holloway! They meant to make sure of 'er."

A babble of argument began among the spectators. Many shared the sailor's indignation. Others were delighted that for once the authorities had been too smart for the suffragettes. Mrs Pankhurst should be locked up again until she had served the rest of her sentence.

Belle seethed inwardly. She had never been quite clear about what Mrs Pankhurst was supposed to have done. Some women – never caught, never even identified – had blown up a house that was being built for Mr Lloyd George, a cabinet minister who was the implacable enemy of the suffragettes. Mrs Pankhurst had known nothing beforehand, even the prosecution admitted that she had been nowhere near the scene of the outrage, but she had been blamed for it. "As an accessory", apparently, because of her militant views. Three years' imprisonment, if Belle remembered right, had been her sentence at the Old Bailey.

Belle knew now, quite certainly, where her own sympathies lay. That brief encounter with Mrs Pankhurst had completed the process started on Epsom racecourse six months ago.

The tug had cast off, gone surging away, its tall funnel belching black smoke. A new chugging sound was audible as another, smaller craft rounded the bows of the *Majestic*. Two women stood up, wearing sashes that proclaimed them as suffragettes. Their voices rang thinly through the keen air. Other women, in the stern, were shouting too.

"Cats are here, Mrs Pankhurst! They're close on you!"

There was a derisive chorus from the rail. "Too

17

late, my dears!" "The cats have got her – and a good thing too!"

For a few moments the message did not penetrate. The two women were still shouting their useless warning as they passed beneath the spot where Belle was standing. She felt a pang of compassion as she looked down. They stood so straight, so resolute, amid the driving spray. One was middle-aged, in a big hat she had been forced to secure with a scarf knotted beneath her chin. The other, a girl like herself, wore a cape with a hood that had been blown back to reveal her head, with dark hair tousled by the wind, a nose and chin like sculpture.

Then the news of Mrs Pankhurst's arrest got through to them. The fishing boat veered away, abandoning its useless mission, and headed back to port.

There was nothing to be done, Mrs Blake and her friends dejectedly agreed. The police were probably heading, the skipper explained, for some private landing place along the coast, where it would be illegal to follow them. In any case, what could a few ladies do against them?

"We are not a violent movement," said Mrs Blake patiently. "We do not believe in violence."

Fiona noticed that the unknown young man was listening with particular interest. The ladies plunged into a vigorous discussion. What about the great rally planned for Sunday? How could

18

they "welcome home" their leader if she was not on the platform?

"It can be a protest meeting," said Mrs Blake. "We shall have plenty to protest about," she added grimly.

The immediate need was to telephone headquarters and report what had happened. Then, after a quick cup of coffee to warm them up, back to London on the first train. By now their craft was nosing its way expertly into its berth. After settling for its hire they headed for the hotel close by, where they had spent the night.

"Will you order the coffee, Miss Campbell, while I telephone?"

"Certainly, Mrs Blake."

Fiona hurried away. When she returned she found her companions sitting rather morosely round a table. Mrs Blake alone was standing, fidgeting impatiently. "The telephone appears to be engaged," she said crossly.

"Do sit down," said Fiona. "I'll fetch you the moment it's free."

"You're very good, my dear. I won't refuse."

Fiona recrossed the hall and found the telephone in its dark little cubbyhole under the stairs. She could hear a man's voice speaking with slow deliberation. Through the glass she recognized the stranger in the boat. It *would* be him, she thought irritably. He would somehow get here ahead of us.

He was speaking at what, in her office, old Mr Bagshaw termed "dictation speed". Perhaps the young man was himself making a long-distance call, for he was articulating each word very distinctly. She stepped back a pace or two, out of politeness, but could not help hearing what he said.

"The welcome home meeting will become a protest rally." The voice changed to a conversational tone. "That's the end of the copy. Mr Rudd knows I'll be in touch if I find out anything more. I'm catching the next train to Exeter." He paused briefly. Then he said, "Dangerfield, Guy Dangerfield."

She must fetch Mrs Blake. As she turned, the door clicked open behind her and the voice greeted her pleasantly.

"Ah, just the person I wanted!"

She resented his familiar tone. "I can't stop – I was beginning to think you were something to do with the police."

"Nothing like that. But if I could ask you a few questions—"

"You've no right. You'd no right to be in our boat. You're a journalist," she accused him. "Spying on us."

"Oh, *come*." He was barring her way to the coffee room. "I've got the names of all the others, I just need yours. And in your case – I don't think it would be offensive, do you? – if I enquired your age as well?" She wondered afterwards if there had not been a hint of admiration mixed with the impertinence, but she was in no mood to hesitate.

"It *is* offensive, very offensive." She had taken off her gloves, and the impact of her bare palm on his cheek rang through the foyer.

A few minutes later the experienced Mrs Blake was calming her with coffee. "Understandable, my dear, but seldom advisable, to slap a journalist across the face!"

CHAPTER THREE

Guy Dangerfield had taken the assault remarkably well.

It was an experience anyhow, he reflected as he made for the railway station. He had been slapped in the face by a girl before, but not since he was nine and the girl a hefty eleven-year-old. This latest experience was quite different. And was it not experience that he was seeking?

Six months ago, when his first novel came out, he had been stung by one reviewer: *"Mr Dangerfield has wit and a way with words, but only Time will cure his principal weakness – he has just not lived long enough yet. Before attempting a second novel this promising young writer would be wise to wait until..."*

His publisher had tried to soothe him. "Something in it, me boy. Perhaps a *leetle* more experience, don't you know?" He recommended journalism. Gave one an insight into many different walks of life. And the money might be useful. Unless a first novelist was lucky it could be years before book royalties gave him a livelihood.

Obediently, Guy scoured Fleet Street for work. Vainly. He was told that a young man must start in the provinces and learn his trade the hard way. But Guy did not want to go back to the provinces. London was where everything happened and where the publishers were.

Surely *one* of the city's evening newspapers, if none of the nationals, could use a "promising young writer" with "wit and a way with words"? Apparently not. Weary and dejected, he came to the eighth and humblest paper on his list. Fortunately its Mr Rudd was, like himself, from Yorkshire.

Even that friendly little man could not invent a non-existent job for him. "But there are bits and pieces, lad. I'm always on the look-out for them. The staff men can't be everywhere. I'll always look at anything you send in." He held out a press ticket for a recital by an obscure pianist. "Might be worth a couple of paras. Not more."

So Guy was launched upon a career of grubbing for odd guineas. Sometimes Rudd took his copy, sometimes not. And there were those occasions when no staff man was available, so the pay was certain and he might get a free theatre or concert ticket into the bargain. He was brought into contact with all sorts of people, getting a wider vision of the world.

"Good idea to specialize a bit as well," one man advised him. "Get known as the chap who knows a thing or two about the background."

Guy observed that Rudd had a certain sympathy with these women who were always agitating for votes. Well, not sympathy, maybe – pressmen had to be impartial – but an "interest". "They're always up to something outlandish," said Rudd defensively. "Good for a headline. So – any good story you can bring me on the suffragettes, I'll likely buy it."

He had done so on several occasions. And the Plymouth story, he had assured Guy, was a real scoop. Besides the brief factual report Guy had just dictated for today's later editions, he wanted a full-length descriptive piece of that dash across Plymouth Sound. It would be an exclusive in tomorrow's issue, with Guy's name on it, his first byline ever.

Guy was already scribbling down his copy as the express glided into Exeter. He broke his journey there just long enough to check the accuracy of his own guess – Mrs Pankhurst had arrived and was safely lodged in Exeter jail. The agencies would be handling the story from now on. He hurried back to the station, bought a sandwich, and caught the next London train.

He resumed the rough draft of his feature. One thing worried him – he wanted to highlight that suffragette girl, standing erect in the bows, decorative as a figurehead. "And you didn't get her *name*?" Rudd would demand. "Her age? Her background? Was she a *Londoner*? What sort of a journalist do you call yourself?" Guy shuddered to imagine himself answering feebly, "I asked her – but she only slapped my face."

Reluctantly he decided that he must play down her part in the drama. He finished his piece, read it back, trimmed it to the length Rudd wanted. Then, having travelled down on a very early train, he tilted over in his corner and caught up on his sleep.

Walking out of Paddington he saw, daubed across the pavement at his bus stop in large white letters:

WELCOME HOME RALLY FOR MRS PANKHURST
EMPRESS THEATRE
SUNDAY

Two earnest-looking women were blotting out the first two words and substituting PROTEST. They were quick off the mark, he thought admiringly. The newspaper-boys were still racing along Praed Street yelling, "Pankhurst sensation! Arrest at sea!"

Darkness had fallen, though Oxford Street was an unbroken dazzle of pre-Christmas window-display. He jumped off at Holborn, plunged through the dimmer byways round Red

Lion Square, and reached Lamb's Conduit Street, where the friendly little shops near his flat produced the illusion of living in a village. He paused to buy sausages, then let himself into the gloomy gas-lit hall, and climbed the stairs. His flat was three flights up, through a pervasive atmosphere of perpetually heating cat food from the old couple's kitchen just below him. He tried to forget the cat food as he laid out the pallid sausages in his frying pan and pricked them with a fork. They were soon sizzling cheerfully and turning to a healthier brown. The kettle started to sing.

The gas fire made everything more cheerful. When he had eaten and coaxed the last cupful of tea from the pot, he would willingly have lain back and slipped into sleep. But he must type his copy and take it down to Fleet Street, ready for tomorrow's midday edition.

He groaned, uncovered his typewriter and began to tap away with two fingers. Then out into the chilly dark, a brisk walk down Chancery Lane and into Fleet Street, where the presses of the national dailies were throbbing away to produce next morning's papers. Rudd had gone, his own final edition safely on the streets. Guy handed in his piece and strode home.

What a day, what an endless day! Bed at last – no, a bath first. A match scraped, the geyser lit with its usual alarming explosion, the arc of steaming water came hissing down. He lay and wallowed, and thought again of that girl.

Rudd had said nothing about covering the Sunday rally in the Empress Theatre. Might be a good idea to go there, see what happened... Might get a paragraph out of it... Or something.

CHAPTER FOUR

Fiona too was looking forward to Sunday's meeting.

Their failure to save Mrs Pankhurst from arrest had been a cruel disappointment. But even her absence from the platform at Earl's Court would not rob the rally of its emotional quality. Fiona would not have missed it for anything.

It was also a perfect excuse for cutting short her weekend visit to her home in the south London suburbs. Normally, as soon as her office closed at midday on Saturdays, she was expected to rush for her train at Victoria – and stay till Sunday evening or even crack of dawn on Monday. She loved her mother, she was willing to share her sister's bed, but her stepfather's company was increasingly irksome.

"Uncle Jim", as she still called him, was not even a real uncle. He had come into the house as a lodger, and remained when her father went off to the South African war. His weekly payment was more badly needed than ever when her father died in the military hospital in Cape Town. After a decent interval Uncle Jim had married her mother. Fiona could never accept him as a substitute parent. The job in central London had provided her means of escape.

"But he's *fond* of you," her mother would protest. Fiona did not like the ways he showed his affection – the bear-like hugs, the reek of whisky on the rough moustache scraping across her lips, the heavy humour when he twitted her about her friends.

That particular Saturday he had picked up a new music hall song in the pub. He set the kitchen ringing with it when he came blundering in.

"Put me on an island where the girls are few,
Put me with the most ferocious lions in the zoo,
Put me on a treadmill, and I'll never, never fret –
But for pity's sake don't put me with a Suffragette!"

"Don't worry," said Fiona tartly, "I'm just off to bed. *I've* had a hard week."

She had said nothing about the Plymouth adventure. There was no hope now of continuing the quiet chat with her mother. She gave her a goodnight kiss, slid skilfully past Uncle Jim and ran upstairs. She heard his laughter below.

29

"What that gal wants is a young man to knock some sense into her!"

Soon after breakfast she slipped thankfully away. Her mother could not comprehend why she was missing Sunday dinner just for some meeting. Surely the Sunday roast, with all the trimmings on which Uncle Jim insisted, should be a landmark in the weekly round of cheap teashop lunches and makeshift suppers with that girl who shared her rooms? Fiona herself felt a pang of regret as she hurried to the station, the grey air full of clanging church bells, the grey streets full of grey people parading to church and chapel.

She lunched frugally in the refreshment room at Victoria, reached Earl's Court in ample time, donned her sash, drew her collection-plate, and was allotted her area in the auditorium. She stood in the foyer, fascinated to study the variety of types attracted to the suffragette cause. There were grand ladies, descending from motorcars or carriages, bowing their heads in stately fashion lest their immense hats be knocked askew. There were East End factory-girls in shawls, with pinched white faces. There were clever-looking intellectual women – she spotted Doctor Ethel Smyth, in her mannish tweeds, who had taken time from composing her operas to give the movement its stirring *March of the Women*. There were a lot of men too – escorts and serious sympathizers and possibly troublemakers. In top hats and trilbies, bowlers and cloth caps, they streamed across the foyer.

A diffident voice murmured in her ear. She swung round. "I'm sorry?"

"I was just asking, what do we do to join?"

It was a girl of her own age, fair, a pink and gold girl, expensively dressed.

"You can fill in a form. From that table." Fiona led her across and hovered, ready to help. The girl bent forward and wrote.

"*Isherwood*," Fiona read, "*Isabel Florence*." Then the girl gave a little cry of vexation. "Dash! Force of habit!" She crossed out the word she had just written below and substituted "*Miss*". Fiona saw that the word crossed out was "*Lady*". She exclaimed in turn when the next space was filled in with "*63 Bedford Square*".

"Oh – we're almost neighbours!"

The stranger's smile was radiant. "Really? *You* live in the square?"

"Lord, no!" Fiona thought of the stately eighteenth-century houses she passed every day on her way to the office. "Nothing so grand! A little side street, Francis Street, just off Tottenham Court Road—"

"I know! By that interesting furniture shop! I adore those simple modern designs, don't you?" They clearly had tastes in common. But when she had signed her form the girl said, with an obvious effort: "Don't think me rude – but when I saw you just now I wondered, haven't I seen

31

you before? Was it you, on Thursday, in that motorboat? At Plymouth?"

"I *was* in a motorboat – at Plymouth – "

"And *I* was on deck on the *Majestic*! I'd been talking to Mrs Pankhurst, actually." The girl's voice thrilled with pride. "I saw them arrest her."

Fiona longed to hear more. "Are you alone?" she asked.

"Yes. Mamma wanted my brother to come with me, but you know what brothers are – "

"We must find you a seat." Fiona led the way up the stairs. She saw two empty places at the end of a row. "I must be on the gangway," she explained. "Got to jump up in the interval with my collecting-plate."

For a few minutes they compared notes excitedly about the Plymouth episode. Belle seemed thrilled to meet someone so deeply involved in the adventure. Fiona envied her that encounter with Mrs Pankhurst. She herself had never seen her at close quarters, much less spoken to her. "But she's always in prison," she said. "Like now."

The theatre was packed. There must have been four or five thousand people. A cheer went up as someone was carried in on a stretcher and placed in a prominent position in front.

"That's Annie Kenney," Fiona whispered. "She's been on hunger-strike." Annie was a Lancashire mill-girl, she explained, and still often wore her shawl. She had heard Mrs Pankhurst's eldest daughter speak, and fallen under her spell. Christabel Pankhurst had brought her down to London. Annie had little education but she soon proved herself a born organizer. She was now one of the best-loved figures in the movement.

"Those hunger-strikes – I don't know how they can do it." Belle shuddered. "I wouldn't have the courage."

"I don't think *I* would." Fiona knew that she was not cut out for martyrdom. She had never deliberately sought arrest as some women did. If she appeared in court, let alone was sent to jail, she would lose her job. And new ones were not easy to find. Arrest would mean not only a few weeks in prison, it would mean a humiliating return home, to be a financial burden on her mother and a butt for Uncle Jim's crude humour.

A diminutive figure was advancing, with something like a swagger, to the front of the stage. She was met with an almost hysterical ovation.

"Who on earth is *she*?" Belle demanded.

"That's the General."

"The *what*?"

"That's what we call her. Mrs Flora Drummond."

Belle soon saw that the nickname was appropriate. Her speech, delivered in broad Scots, was brisk and confident, carrying the very accent of command. Each decisive sentence was met with an outburst of applause. Fiona, longing to tell her new friend about this legendary character, knew that she must wait for a quieter occasion.

Flora Drummond might not look like a general. Barely five feet tall, she had once missed a Post Office job by being an inch below the regulation minimum. She had earned her nickname for her organizing talents and a fighting spirit inherited from her Highland ancestors.

As a heckler she could hold her own – even against Winston Churchill, who as Home Secretary had been a formidable opponent of the suffragettes. And once, outside 10 Downing Street, while the police were occupied with a woman who had chained herself to the railings, the General had accidentally touched an innocent-looking knob on the Prime Minister's front door. To her delighted surprise it had activated a catch and the door had swung open. Before anyone could stop her, the General had marched in – and it had taken several horrified private secretaries to eject her.

Over the past few years there had been no end to her exploits. She had hired a motorboat on the Thames and, with a megaphone, harangued the MPs as they sat at tea on their famous terrace. Just before George the Fifth's coronation she had led a rival procession astride an immense charger, wearing a peaked military cap and a long riding coat with epaulettes. Surely Belle had heard of her?

Today the General was recruiting ladies for a bodyguard which in future would surround Mrs

34

Pankhurst and protect her from arrest. Even a small woman, if she studied the Japanese art of jujitsu, could overthrow a strong man.

This suggestion met with enthusiasm from some of the audience but disapproval from others. "It could be dangerous," said the woman on Belle's far side. "You could injure someone – even kill him."

The General wound up her speech with an appeal for funds. "There will now be an interval – during which the collectors will go round. Think of the leader we should be welcoming home today. Give generously!"

Fiona sprang up and hurried away to the area assigned to her.

CHAPTER FIVE

Coins pattered into her plate. Copper, silver, often gold. There were discreetly folded banknotes. There were rings and other items of jewellery. One old woman dropped in a shabby, clinking little bag that probably contained farthings. Fiona moved smiling along the rows, but never looked straight at the giver or the gift so as to cause embarrassment.

She would have passed Guy Dangerfield without recognizing him if he had not mumbled awkwardly: "Press. We're supposed to be neutral."

"Of course." She saw then who it was. "Oh, it's *you*!" Her face went hot as she remembered the slap. "I owe you an apology – I was so ashamed afterwards!"

"Think nothing of it." He had a rather attractive smile.

Someone was waiting to pass. "I – I mustn't block the way – " She moved along, stumbling over people's feet.

"See you later," he called after her.

There was no need. She had made her apology. She completed her collection, handed in the result and returned thankfully to Belle.

Several speakers followed. The last was a recent hunger-striker – only one of hundreds, she emphasized, who had taken this desperate action in the past year. "People say, surely it is all folly. If it is not hysteria, at least it is unreasonable. Unreasonable? They will not realize that we are like an army, we fight for a cause, and in a struggle weapons must be used. The weapons we ask for are simple – a fair hearing – but that is refused us in Parliament, refused us by the government, refused us in the law courts. Men would choose violence, but the women of this movement have stood out against killing – or even harming their opponents. They prefer to endure the horrors of the hunger-strike themselves, and exert moral pressure on the government – "

This statement produced a roar of applause, not least from Belle's neighbour. The speaker wound up with a fervent appeal. "This is the most glorious fight that has ever been! Before you leave this theatre, become a member of our Union. Say, 'I will stand by you whatever the world says, whatever public opinion says!' Say you are for us – *now* – before another minute goes by!" Belle was shouting with the rest.

The woman walked shakily from the platform.

As the tumult subsided someone came forward and stirred it up afresh with an announcement. The collection had amounted to more than ten thousand pounds. With the funds raised by Mrs Pankhurst's meetings in America the total would be almost fifteen thousand. But they would need every penny for the struggle that now lay ahead.

As the two girls went down the stairs, Belle said, "Since we both live in Bloomsbury, perhaps – "

"Of course! Let's go together."

The young man stood waiting in the foyer. "It's for me to apologize – accosting you like that at Plymouth—"

Belle broke in. "Plymouth? It was you in the motorboat?"

"You'll excuse us, we have to catch our bus," said Fiona coolly. She sailed on, leaving Belle to follow. He must not get Belle's name and put it in his paper.

They boarded a bus. "Can we go on the top?" Belle pleaded.

"Why not?"

They climbed the curving stairs, managing their skirts as best they could. It was chilly on the open upper deck. Fiona unclipped the waterproof apron and spread it over their laps.

"What a good idea!" Belle had seldom been on a bus and never, she confessed, by herself. This airy voyage, sailing along high above the crowded pavements, was almost an adventure.

"But how did you come?" asked Fiona, amused.

"The butler whistled up a taxi. Mamma gave me the fare for another back." She laughed. "I put it in the collection! Oh, I've got enough for the bus – but I'd never have known *which* bus."

The conductor came clattering up the stairs. The journalist had followed them and found a seat close by. He might try to pay for them. Fiona was determined to prevent that. She fixed the conductor with a firm eye and held out a sixpence.

"Where to, miss?"

In her haste she had not chosen the most convenient bus for her new friend. Still, if they got off at the top of Tottenham Court Road she could walk on with her as far as Bedford Square.

The young man got off at the same stop. She had felt sure he would. "You seem to be following us," she said lightly.

"No. I gather you both live in Bloomsbury. So do I. Lamb's Conduit Street."

That was the furthest edge of Bloomsbury. Certainly he had not taken the most convenient bus. They could hardly shake him off as they walked down Tottenham Court Road.

"May I introduce myself?" he said. "Guy Dangerfield."

She was forced to say, "My name's Campbell. And this is Miss Isherwood."

"I would bow – but it might look silly." They were more at ease now, chattering as they walked, exchanging memories of Thursday.

"This is a *lovely* coincidence," said Belle. She added, regretfully, "I do wish I could ask you in for a rather late cup of tea, but…"

Thank God she's got some sense, thought Fiona. The fat would be in the fire. Bringing home two complete strangers! I'd be bad enough – quite unacceptable socially. But a man! A journalist!

She too however was reluctant to break off this conversation. At the corner of Francis Street she said: "This is where *I* live. If you'd like a cup of tea, Belle—"

"Oh, please!" Belle's delight was obvious.

"I live over that laundry."

A conventional young man might have made his farewells, raised his hat and walked tactfully away into the night. She had a feeling that Mr Dangerfield would not.

"Do you realize," he said, "that by now Mrs Pankhurst is almost certainly out of prison?"

Who could possibly break up the party after that?

They fired questions at him as they climbed the stairs. Luckily Fiona's room-mate Daisy was not yet back from her weekend at home, so there was no call for introductions or explanations.

Guy had picked up the news in a Fleet Street pub. The government no longer dared to subject Mrs Pankhurst to forcible feeding and they were terrified of her dying on their hands when she went on hunger-strike. She would be held in Exeter jail just long enough to miss the meeting. "She's probably in the train by now," he said.

There was some advantage, Fiona had to admit, in knowing a newspaper man.

Belle was asking him what had made him want to be one. "I don't," he corrected her. "It's a stop-gap. I want to be a novelist." His first effort had come out not long ago.

"I say! What's it called?"

"*The Anvil.* Because that's how your character is formed. Blows of Fate, and all that."

Belle was scribbling down the title. She's going to *buy* it, thought Fiona. But her sort could afford to buy books. "You should write a novel about suffragettes," she said.

"I don't think a novelist should make propaganda."

"What about Dickens?" She cut into the cake that, most conveniently, her mother had baked for her. "And H.G. Wells? *Ann Veronica*'s about suffragettes."

"And other things," said Belle with her gurgly laugh. "At school we were forbidden to read it."

"It's about the New Woman," said Fiona, "at the dawn of this twentieth century."

There was much to talk about. Belle looked at her wristwatch and cried out in horror. "Mamma will think I've got myself arrested! May I use your telephone?"

Fiona explained with a smile that she did not possess one or know any private home that did.

41

"Never mind. I'll just have to run."

Guy leapt to his feet. "I'll see you safely back."

"So will I," Fiona insisted. Too late she wondered if this had been a welcome offer. At the moment, however, she was more concerned about the extra disapproval Belle might incur if she was seen with this unknown young man.

They fairly raced the short distance to Bedford Square. On the last street-corner Belle panted a hurried goodbye. "I must pretend I had a long wait for a taxi!"

"And now," said Guy cheerfully, turning to Fiona, "I must see *you* home again."

"Nonsense," she told him. "You have your piece to write for the paper. You said so. I walk these streets every day of my life. I am a working woman. I am independent. I am H.G. Wells's New Woman!"

"All right." He grinned down at her and she grinned back. "Good night, Ann Veronica. And thanks for the cake!"

CHAPTER SIX

There were mornings when Guy's newspaper made him explode over his breakfast, sometimes with laughter, sometimes with the violence of indignation.

On the day that he read Lady Bathurst's statement to the press it was a mixture of the two. "*When a suffragette has been convicted,*" the lady declared, "*first have her well birched (by women), then shave off her hair, and finally deport her to Australia or New Zealand.*" She had suggested these countries presumably because both had granted votes to women some years earlier.

If I were a girl, thought Guy, I know how *I* should feel. He had been quite impartial – indeed, not especially interested – when he had drifted almost by accident into this field of topical controversy. After attending a few meetings, and especially now that he had made the acquaintance

43

of Fiona and Belle, his sympathy was developing fast.

His inside information about Mrs Pankhurst had been accurate. She had been released from Exeter, but too late to appear at the rally. Now the talk in Fleet Street was that she had fled to Paris. Guy was puzzled. That woman was a fighter, not the sort to run away. The puzzle was solved when he learnt that she had crossed the Channel only to consult with her daughter Christabel about the tactics for the next stage in the campaign.

He had never seen Christabel. She was permanently in Paris because the British government could not touch her there. She was famous for her good looks and her brains – she was said, indeed, to be the brains of the movement. She held a first-class degree in law, had won a special prize for international law, but of course – being a mere female – she was not allowed to practise in a British court. A year or two ago, when suffragettes were being arrested right and left, the police had scoured the country for her. Guy, though he had then little interest in the subject, could still remember the press sensation, the cartoons and comic verses that had made her a popular heroine. One jingle lived in his memory:

They seek her here, they seek her there,
Detectives prowling everywhere.

Finally she had turned up in Paris, where, as a lawyer, she knew that the French would treat her as a political refugee and not allow the British to extradite her. From this place of safety she edited the movement's weekly paper.

Who would have blamed Mrs Pankhurst, thought Guy, if she had stayed in Paris and shared her daughter's immunity? But his assessment of her character had been accurate. Her ticket-of-leave was for seven days and she would be liable for rearrest from Sunday onwards. And the word now was that she would return to London on Saturday. As her followers had been denied the chance to welcome her home last Sunday he felt sure they would make up for it at Victoria Station. There might even be a first appearance of the General's female bodyguard.

An occasion he must not miss.

The same idea had occurred to many others. Crowds were milling round the station forecourt, clustering in the adjacent streets. The air was electric with expectancy. A railway terminus was always a place where people waited to meet other people. Today there was a difference – nearly all were waiting to meet the same person.

He saw many faces familiar to him from suffragette rallies he had attended. And the police seemed to be extraordinarily numerous.

45

The boat-train was due in twenty minutes. He sauntered innocently towards the arrival platform. There were the usual taxis waiting – but oddly, in the middle of the rank, there was a very powerful-looking private motorcar. Two men sat in it and a grim-faced, drably-dressed woman behind them. Three uniformed constables stood by the car. Others, straddling motorcycles, were edging their machines into the fringes of the picture.

There was another odd thing. The taxis contained, instead of the usual solitary driver, four men each – always four men, with the massive physique and nondescript headgear of the plain-clothes policeman.

Guy's pulse quickened. He did not like the look of this. Were they expecting disorder? Surely they could not touch Mrs Pankhurst today?

Someone shouted a command. A line of uni-formed men was suddenly strung across the station concourse, advancing and herding people away from the arrival platform.

"Sorry, sir, sorry, madam – we have to clear this side of the station. No, sir, it's everybody, I'm afraid – "

Guy had hoped to get an eye-witness story. He glanced round. How could he elude the advancing cordon? There was one place that policemen would hardly search for skulking suffragettes. He dived down the white-tiled subway, groping for a penny to ensure complete concealment.

He waited five minutes. It was quiet overhead.

He emerged, washed his hands under the eye of the attendant, and climbed the stairs, pausing just short of the top, so that only head and shoulders were in view. A vast empty space stretched to the arrival platform, where figures clustered, peaked caps and bowlers and helmets nodding together. Waiting.

All heads were turned towards the distant sound of the approaching train. Louder and louder ... then a diminuendo as, dead on time, the Dover boat-train glided smoothly into the terminus.

The usual hubbub of chatter and opening doors was quelled by a voice of authority through a megaphone. "All passengers kindly remain in the train! This is a police order. Close the doors, please." There were obedient slams along the train, but from every window curious heads were thrust out.

The waiting figures converged on one of the first-class compartments. Someone – Mrs Pankhurst, Guy could only suppose – was being hustled along the platform. Her voice pealed out in protest. "This is an outrage! You have no right to arrest me today!"

The uniformed constables formed up in a double rank leading to the car. Mrs Pankhurst was bundled into the back. The escorting fleet of taxis had their engines running. The motorcycles roared into life. By the time Guy had run across the concourse the procession was on its way.

The train passengers now began to disembark,

chattering volubly. Guy heard one man explaining: "They got on at the town station in Dover. She'd just been served with tea. She threw the tray straight out of the window!"

"The tea? Why ever—?"

"A hunger-strike starts at the moment of the arrest."

Guy hurried off. He must get to Fleet Street and offer Rudd his story. Without waste of a second. Just outside he almost collided with Fiona Campbell.

"What's happened? They wouldn't let us in."

"They've got Mrs P.! She'll be halfway to Holloway – "

Fiona looked stricken. "Look," he said desperately, "I can't stop – I must get to Fleet Street." An idea struck him. "Come with me! You can sit in the outer office while I write my copy. Then – I know a splendid teashop just off the Strand. I owe you tea and cake from last Sunday!"

He bustled her into a taxi. An hour later, relaxing over their second cup, he said: "I'm sorry if I was rather bossy. But the story *had* to come first."

She laughed. "Of course! So long as you don't think I'm a submissive female. I didn't argue – but not because you're a man. Just then you *were* a journalist, like it or not – and you were doing a worthwhile job."

CHAPTER SEVEN

A week later Fiona received an invitation from Guy Dangerfield. He had two press tickets for the opera, a royal gala performance, which would mean dressing up.

She had no evening dress, but her flatmate worked in an Oxford Street store and had a wardrobe out of all proportion to her modest wage. Fortunately their measurements were the same.

"I'll lend you my fish dress," Daisy suggested.

"Would you really?"

The fish silhouette had been all the rage last year. Even now, at the end of 1913, it was as near the height of fashion as ordinary mortals would hope to attain. Daisy's dress was a dinner gown with sleeves, the bodice boldly cut down in a great revealing V almost to the (fortunately) high waist. The long draped skirt would swish importantly down a theatre gangway. The dress was lemon yellow, with a tiny sprinkled pattern.

"It's *you*," said Daisy.

Next day, to Fiona's embarrassment, came a second invitation, by hand – also for the opera, on the same evening. It came from Flora Drummond, and was not so much an invitation as a command. It was just a duplicated slip. *"Look forward to seeing you there. An appeal will be delivered to HM during the first interval and must be supported from all sides. Ticket enclosed. Bring own banner."*

The ticket was for the gallery. "HM" must signify King George the Fifth. The government was refusing to accept petitions from mere women as they were not "electors" but, as Christabel Pankhurst cleverly argued, they were undeniably "subjects" and were entitled to petition their king. This gala performance was an opportunity to do so with maximum publicity.

Fiona was proud to be included in this enterprising plan, but it was cruelly disappointing that it clashed with Guy Dangerfield's invitation.

"Well, *you* can't be in it," said Daisy decidedly. "*You* can't jump up in the stalls waving a banner. There's the young man to consider."

"I wouldn't dream of causing him embarrassment. But –" Fiona hesitated. "I needn't let Mrs Drummond down either."

"I don't see—"

"This is all planned for the first interval. It could be over in ten minutes. If I slip out of my seat and

50

run upstairs to join the others, nobody will spot me from the stalls. And by the end of the interval I can be back in my seat as cool as a cucumber." Even as she said this, she thought it sounded distinctly optimistic.

Luckily the banner would be only a small square of calico with VOTES FOR WOMEN boldly printed on it. It was usually quite easy to hide until needed. Neatly folded or tightly rolled it would go under a winter coat or a blouse. Evening dress was more of a problem, but she would wear a wrap against the December night. And once the banner had served its purpose she could lose it somehow on her way back to the stalls.

The young man called for her with a taxi. She went downstairs carefully, mindful of that gorgeous skirt rustling round her heels.

"You look very splendid," he said.

"You look rather distinguished yourself, Mr Dangerfield." He had hired tails for the occasion.

"Do you think tonight we could drop the 'Mr Dangerfield' – and the 'Miss Campbell'?"

She laughed. "I understand that Queen Victoria passed away some years ago. So I think we might – Guy."

She hoped that this harmony would survive the interval.

It was a short ride to Bow Street. There was such a long line of cars and carriages creeping forward to the great porticoed entrance that it seemed better to pay off the taxi and weave their way through the sightseers already thronging the pavement.

Inside, the splendours of the foyer and grand staircase were enhanced by the banked floral displays, the flags and the bunting. Fiona hoped that she looked all right. Everyone else seemed to be sparkling with medals and orders, tiaras and necklets.

They were shown to their stalls. Thank God, she would be able to slip out smartly when the curtain fell. She arranged herself carefully, giving no glimpse of her banner. The red velvet curtains had the royal cipher embroidered in gold. Only the box reserved for the King and Queen was still unoccupied.

"Good heavens!" Guy exclaimed under his breath.

She followed his gaze. Three impressively gowned ladies had entered one of the best boxes, facing that intended for the royal party.

Belle Isherwood looked positively ethereal.

"She's not with her parents," Guy whispered. "I've seen photographs of the Countess."

"So – you know who Belle is?"

"Oh, yes. Lady Isabel, daughter of the Earl of Cleveland. If you work for a paper you learn to do your homework."

She hoped that at least he had no inkling of the planned demonstration. She could not believe that he had. Would Belle be equally taken by surprise?

There was a round of applause as the conductor appeared in the orchestra pit. Then a shivery fanfare, a roll of drums, and the first crashing chords of the national anthem. Everyone rose. She saw the bearded King. Queen Mary passing her bouquet to a lady-in-waiting. Then the house dimmed, the footlights blazed in golden brilliance, and the overture began.

The opera was about Joan of Arc, the words in French, the music unfamiliar. Fiona was conscious of the splendid sound and of the spectacle filling the immense stage, but she could think only of the approaching interval.

At last the curtain fell, the house lights came on, the orchestra crept away out of its pit. Tense and dry-mouthed, she slipped from her seat, paused only to whisper reassuringly in Guy's ear, "Soon be back!" and fled for the upper gallery. The endless stairs were awkward in that skirt. The fashionable fish silhouette was not designed for speed.

Panting, she reached the gallery. Someone far below – goodness, it was one of Belle's companions! – was standing up in her box, and addressing the startled King through a megaphone.

"Women are fighting even today, as Joan of Arc fought centuries ago, for liberty! They are being tortured, their lives put at risk, in *your* name, Your Majesty, and by the orders of *your* ministers – "

In the stalls people were shouting in shocked voices. "Disgraceful!" "Throw her out!" The bald heads and the elaborate coiffures tossed with indignation like a storm-lashed sea.

King George stared back at the speaker, seemingly paralyzed. In the gallery, round Fiona, there was equal uproar.

"Why doesn't someone *do* something? Get them out!"

"They've locked themselves in!"

"They've barricaded the door!"

The amplified voice went on remorselessly. Then came a furious battering in the background, a crash as the door yielded, a rush of dark figures.

The Queen was plucking at the King's sleeve. He rose. They left the royal box, followed by a flurry of scandalized courtiers.

Belle also, and her companions, were lost to sight in a scrum of indignant attendants. Their exit was assisted with less ceremony.

Meanwhile, all over the gallery, hitherto quiet and well-behaved women were producing their little square banners of white calico. Leaflets were sailing down like snowflakes into the dress circle and stalls. Fiona ran to the brass rail of the gallery and flapped her own banner with zeal.

Furious arguments were raging in every part of the opera house. It was three-quarters of an hour before the performance could continue. Long before that she had rejoined Guy.

She was relieved to see a distinct twinkle in his eye. "I won't ask where you've been," he said.

"Are you cross? Should I have warned you?"

"Of course not."

"I wonder what's happened to Belle. Fancy *her*! She only joined at the Earl's Court meeting."

"I expect her name helped – in getting that box."

The second interval was much shorter. He bought her a glass of white wine. "You need it. I think you deserve it."

Her anxiety on Belle's account was soon relieved. They met one of Guy's journalist friends. No one was being charged, he said. The police disliked arresting people with titles and social influence. These suffragettes only wanted more publicity. Why give it to them?

"A coward's excuse!" said Fiona. She enjoyed the rest of the evening.

CHAPTER
EIGHT

"Those wild women! In front of the King and Queen! What's the world coming to?" Fiona kept her face blank as Mr Bagshaw scowled at the headlines.

His office in Red Lion Square was almost pure Dickens. She herself, one of the few modern additions, was still referred to as his "typewriter". But she gave satisfaction. Her spelling was faultless, she had mastered the unfamiliar legal terms, she was – unlike her employer – at ease with the new-fangled telephone, which she would answer calmly, not as though it were a spitting wildcat. Being female, though not flighty, she did not of course smoke, so she did not disappear as the clerks did to puff a furtive cigarette in the storeroom. In short, Mr Bagshaw had decided that Miss Campbell was a good thing, well worth her pound a week, the same rate as the Civil Service. A man would have expected three.

Fiona did not complain. The job had brought freedom – escape from the constraints of home, first to a working girls' hostel, then to the fuller liberty of the attic rooms she shared with Daisy. And the job was safe, so long as she concealed her suffragette sympathies.

Guy, however, was beginning to feel dissatisfied with his journalistic efforts. He wanted to get back to more literary work. His heart leapt one morning when he received a letter, its crested envelope addressed with elaborate loops and flourishes, a positive arabesque in sepia ink. The note inside was similarly decorative.

"Dear Mr Dangerfield, I have just read The Anvil *with immense enjoyment. A real discovery. I look forward to your next novel. Before then, though, I am curious to meet the author. I am At Home every Thursday evening..."* The signature, equally ornate, was *"Ottoline Morrell"* – 44 Bedford Square! That must be quite close to Belle's.

He had heard of Lady Ottoline. Who had not? Wife of an obscure Liberal MP, but sister of the Duke of Portland. Not political, but passionately interested in the arts, friend of the famous, patron of the unknown. An invitation from her meant that you had arrived, or at least were definitely on your way.

Even Rudd was impressed. He himself seldom went anywhere. He spent his life crouched over his desk, a shirt-sleeved spider wreathed in tobacco smoke. But he knew all about those At Homes.

Her ladyship was eccentric, unconventional, insatiably interested in people. Anyone could be drawn into her net. Guy might meet eminent statesmen or hungry geniuses.

He settled one doubt for Guy. "Don't worry about clothes!" Lady Ottoline liked people to dress as they pleased. She was original in her own taste, sometimes with bizarre results. Rudd quoted a famous writer's description of her hat as a crimson tea cosy trimmed with hedgehogs. "Of course, you'll see tail coats and white ties – but plenty of casual Bohemian wear, velvet jackets and so on."

Guy played for safety. When Thursday evening came he presented himself in his best suit, but with a soft-collared shirt and full-flowing, poetic-looking tie like one he had seen in a photograph of Rupert Brooke.

A parlour-maid received him, took his overcoat and hat, and led him through green double doors to a wide hall, from which a curving staircase led up to the drawing room. He mounted it, unusually dry-mouthed and nervous.

The drawing room was a vast double room, running from front to back of the house. It was already crowded and noisy with a dozen animated conversations. There were masses of golden chrysanthemums in huge urns.

He glanced round. What hope of seeing anyone he knew! A few faces were familiar from the newspapers. That must be the great Nijinsky. He had actually *seen* him, dancing in the Ballets Russes. And Lady Ottoline herself was unmistakable.

She stood by the fireplace, tall, with a cloud of mahogany-red hair, high-arched nose, and jaw like the prow of a galley. She wore an embroidered Russian blouse. Perhaps in honour of Nijinsky. She was talking to a lanky man with a long beard, also red-brown, and a solemn cadaverous face. He had an odd squeaky voice and was convulsing her with his wit.

She suddenly became aware of Guy and took a step towards him, thrusting out her hand. "You must be Guy Dangerfield?"

"Yes – you were kind enough – "

She turned to her bearded companion. "Lytton, this is Mr Dangerfield – he's just written a *most* amusing novel. And this," she told Guy, "is Mr Lytton Strachey. You know, of course, his wonderful *Landmarks in French Literature*."

"Of course!" Guy hoped that his lie would not be exposed.

But after a brief civility Mr Strachey said he had just seen someone named Virginia, and must speak to her. He drifted away. "You have no drink," said Lady Ottoline. She signalled to a maid. "Champagne?"

"Thank you."

"It makes my head ache," she said regretfully. She seemed to be sucking a peppermint. "You look younger than I expected." She asked about his next book. He dared not admit that it was not yet started. He said, carefully, "It's still in its *very* early stages – "

"Ah, still evolving! To discuss it with other people can be *fatal*. I know how the creative mind works." She made some intelligent comments on *The Anvil* and asked him about himself. Her sympathy warmed him. He grew in confidence. "I like to watch the careers of young writers," she said. "Do you know the work of D.H. Lawrence?"

"*Sons and Lovers*? I – I've not read it – yet."

"You must. Another young man of promise. But he made me so homesick."

"Homesick?"

"He's from Nottinghamshire – where I grew up. Welbeck Abbey is quite near the pit where his father worked. The dialogue of his characters takes me back into my childhood. I'm dying to meet him. But I gather he lives in Italy."

Guy felt that this was enough about Mr Lawrence. It would be nice to get back to Mr Dangerfield.

But Lady Ottoline was glancing towards the door. "Here's Belle Isherwood. Such a delightful girl. She'll be thrilled to meet you. And I owe it entirely to her recommendation – "

He felt a slight pang of disappointment. So he too owed this to Belle. Lady Ottoline would never have heard of him, otherwise. Clearly Belle had not revealed that she already knew him. Their hostess was introducing them as strangers. He avoided

Belle's eye. He ought to be grateful to her. She was obviously trying to help him.

"I will surrender him to you," said Lady Ottoline in a convincing tone of regret. "I must not neglect my other guests." She sailed away, greeting people effusively in her sonorous, slightly nasal, voice.

Guy could now meet Belle's gaze. "I must thank *you* – "

"You're not cross?" She sounded anxious.

"Of course not! This could be very ... helpful."

"I do hope so."

"Tell me," he whispered, "who some of these people are."

She pointed out Mr Yeats, the Irish poet, with his long hair, pale bow tie, and black-ribboned glasses. He seemed to be declaiming, rather than talking, to a dapper companion, Max Beerbohm, the cartoonist and wit. She identified Ramsay MacDonald, the Labour leader, and a young painter named Stanley Spencer. The woman talking to Mr Strachey was Mrs Woolf, terribly intellectual and to Belle somewhat alarming. She lived close by in Gordon Square. Her set was becoming known as the Bloomsbury Group.

All these clever people, Guy thought, talking so fluently and brilliantly, but – to judge from the scraps of conversation he caught – not about votes for women. This was another world. So much zest and variety. It was an eye-opening experience.

Belle introduced him to a young man of his own age, David Garnett. His father was a publisher's reader, celebrated in literary circles, and his mother well known as the translator of Dostoevsky and other Russian authors. David had stayed with D.H. Lawrence in Austria, just after Lawrence's elopement with Frieda Weekley.

"You should tell Lady Ottoline about them," Guy suggested. "She's very interested in him."

"Oh, I have. Of course, Lawrence is a family friend of ours now. My father's done a lot for him."

Lucky Lawrence, he thought. What it was to have the right kind of friends! But Belle was doing her best for him.

Suddenly she stiffened; her whisper became the hiss of a hostile cat. "See who's here!"

No need to identify the newcomer. That distinguished sculptured head could belong only to the Prime Minister. Mr Asquith crossed the room with outstretched hands to greet his hostess.

"How *can* she?" said Belle between gritted teeth.

"Well, her husband *is* a Liberal."

"She lives her own life! Of course, Asquith knew her as a girl. He was like a favourite uncle, lending her books and everything... But she must know what he's doing now. The arrests – the treatment of the hunger-strikers –" Again Belle became an angry kitten, beautiful but spitting viciously. "I'd like to ask him, in front of everybody, 'Why are you torturing women?' If only I had the nerve."

"You haven't the bad manners, thank God." For an awful moment he had been afraid that perhaps she had.

"No," she admitted. "I'm a guest in this house. It would be unforgivable. And I've been trained," she added bitterly, "to put good manners before anything. But sometimes I think sincerity should come first. Don't worry, Guy." She smiled. "I'm a terrible coward."

By now people were beginning to leave. They went over to thank their hostess for a delightful evening.

"You must come again," she told Guy.

"You were a success," Belle told him as he escorted her the short distance to her own door. "She doesn't say that to everyone." They paused outside her house. "I'm sorry, it's rather late to ask you in. Good night, Guy, and thank you." She squeezed his arm lightly and ran up the steps.

It was not just the lateness of the hour, he knew. She could not walk in and confront her parents with an unknown young man. Mothers of rank had lists of acceptable friends for their daughters. It was advisable to have been at Eton, and then Oxford or Cambridge. Better still, to hold a commission in the Guards. He did not qualify and never would.

That did not trouble him. Striding home to Lamb's Conduit Street he saw a quite different future opening before him.

CHAPTER NINE

A few days later Fiona, making a hurried lunch-hour call at the Kingsway headquarters of the Women's Social and Political Union, was beckoned across by Miss Roe.

Grace Roe had taken over the organizer's post some months earlier – apparently at a moment's notice – when Annie Kenney was sent to prison for eighteen months. In fact, as Fiona now realized, she was well prepared and had been secretly groomed for the work. She was a complete contrast to the Lancashire mill-girl. A soft-spoken young Irishwoman, well educated and, having lost her mother at the age of twelve, already experienced in running a household. Fiona admired her and the way she ran this office.

"Great news," she murmured. "Mrs Pankhurst has dodged the cats. She's in London. Making a public appearance tonight."

Fiona sensed her excitement. "Oh, *where*?"

Miss Roe explained that they dared not hire a hall or advertise the event beforehand. Mrs Pankhurst must not be arrested again. "You know Mouse Castle? She'll speak from that high balcony over the porch."

Mouse Castle was the nickname for 2 Campden Hill Square, home of Mrs Brackenbury, a general's widow and a fearless supporter of the movement. She used it as a refuge for victims of the Cat-and-Mouse Act.

It would have to be an impromptu meeting with whatever crowd they could muster in the square. "But pass the word round," Miss Roe requested. "People you can trust. The vital thing is to get a mention in the newspapers afterwards."

"I'll be there anyhow," Fiona promised.

On her way back to her office she called Belle's telephone number from a public box. An urbane voice answered. "The Earl of Cleveland's residence – " The butler went off to acquaint Lady Isabel. A minute or two later she was on the line, breathless but welcoming. Fiona explained in guarded terms. "You bet!" said Belle. They arranged to meet that evening by the pillar-box in Bedford Square.

Should they tell Guy? Miss Roe was anxious to get something into the papers. He had no telephone, but Fiona, as she walked home from work, could easily make a slight detour by way of Lamb's Conduit Street. So when she left Mr Bagshaw's she hurried through the foggy dusk and rang Guy's bell. It was answered at once by clattering feet on the uncarpeted stairs.

"Fiona!" He looked astonished to see her standing there in the golden ring of the street-lamp.

"I thought you'd like to know – but something confidential – "

"Come in." She followed him upstairs. He said, apologetically, "My place is a bit spartan. I took it unfurnished – so much cheaper, you know."

It was still, to her eye, unfurnished. A rug to cover part of the floorboards, one lumpy old armchair to which he waved her with ceremony, a table on which stood his typewriter – and, draped over a kitchen chair in front of a gas fire, a spotless white shirt. With a cry of horror he snatched it up and fled into another room, which she could only hope, for his sake, contained at least a bed.

"Sorry," he said. "I'm not used to visitors. And my mother made me promise—"

"I know." She laughed. "'Promise me you will always air your clean clothes before you put them on.'"

He stared. "How did you know that?"

"I know mothers."

Her own had said that. She had also said, Fiona remembered suddenly, "Promise me you will never in any circumstances visit a gentleman's rooms by yourself." But, she thought, I am a year older now. And it is 1914.

She told him the time and place of Mrs Pankhurst's planned appearance. He said at once: "Fine! I'll be there."

She stood up. "I must be going. I must go home first, and then I'm meeting Belle..."

He put out an arm to detain her. "You won't have much time. And you must eat something first. I bought some sausages."

She did not argue. He disappeared into some sort of screened-off cubbyhole. She heard him filling a kettle. Soon came the aroma of frizzling sausages. He reappeared briefly, flapped a tablecloth over the space not occupied by his typewriter, and flung down a handful of cutlery. "*Would* you mind?"

"Of course! I expect," she called after his retreating back, "she made you promise never to leave a frying pan?"

"No," he shouted back. "I only learnt that by terrifying experience!"

They were soon sitting down to tea, bread and butter, and sausages. The meal ended with gigantic cream buns from the baker's down the street. "A rather schoolboyish taste, I'm afraid," he said.

"You speak as though your schooldays were prehistoric." He could only have left school three or four years ago.

"Well, quite a bit of history has happened since."

She wondered if he would ever tell her about it. But all too soon it was time to go. He brushed aside her query about the washing-up. As it was, they found Belle already waiting by the pillar-box.

They caught the tube to Notting Hill Gate. In

Campden Hill Square an expectant little crowd had gathered in front of Number Two. Many, thought Fiona, looked like members of Mrs Pankhurst's bodyguard.

They were not kept waiting long. Suddenly the curtains of the first floor windows were flung back. In the light streaming out into the gloom a figure appeared on the wrought-iron balcony above the tall white pillars flanking the front door. There was a burst of welcoming applause as Mrs Pankhurst stepped forward to the rail.

She had been on the run for some time since her last release, staying in safe houses, keeping out of London, lest the police pounce again and send her back to prison to serve another short stretch of her unfinished sentence. But a leader must be seen leading. She could not hide for ever.

She began to speak, quietly and calmly, holding her audience with her extraordinary magnetism.

"My friends, I am here to challenge this cowardly government which makes war on defenceless and voteless women. I have reached London despite armies of police. In a few minutes I am coming out amongst you and I challenge the government to rearrest me!"

Fiona felt something being pushed into her gloved hand. An open notebook. Guy was whispering in her ear. "Could you get me a bit verbatim? Rudd loves a quote."

Obediently she took his pencil and scribbled her shorthand by the light of a street lamp.

Mrs Pankhurst turned to the men in her audience. "I want you men, you taxpayers, to ask what it *costs* to deprive women of the vote – what you pay for these armies of police in plain clothes. Well, if you like to pay, you men who call yourselves practical businessmen, go on paying. You will come to the conclusion that it is cheaper to give women the vote, because I tell you that this fight is going on until we win!"

A furious man began to shout. "You ought to be deported! You're preaching sedition!"

Mrs Pankhurst gave him her sweetest smile. "I should come back again, my friend! Yes, I *am* seditious, and I shall go on being seditious – until I am brought, with other women, within the constitution of my country. For we *have* no constitutional rights, though we are taxed the same as men."

She kept her speech short but vigorous. Fiona felt the tension all around her. Could she finish before the police arrived? Someone would have alerted them by now.

"As the Prime Minister will not listen to us, I have written a letter, a loyal and respectful letter, to the King. I have said to him, 'Your Majesty, we have no power to vote for Members of Parliament, and therefore for us there *is* no House of Commons. We have no voice in the House of Lords. But we *have* a King, and to him we make our appeal. We ask of Your Majesty the audience that we are confident will be granted to us." She wound up amid a tumult of enthusiasm.

Suddenly the balcony was empty. And a minute later she was out on the pavement in the midst of them all, greeting old friends and unknown supporters. Her bodyguard were now much in evidence. Fiona warned Guy not to push forward lest he be mistaken for a plain-clothes policeman.

Within a few minutes the cry was raised. The police *were* coming. Mrs Pankhurst broke free from her admirers and ran into the house. The door slammed behind her. In no time the porch and front steps were packed with a solid phalanx of the bodyguard ladies. Long before they could be shifted Mrs Pankhurst would have made her planned escape through some back way.

The three friends headed for the Underground station. Guy needed a telephone kiosk, to catch the late edition. He dived in, drawing Fiona after him, silencing her confused protests. "I'll need you to read back your shorthand." They stood there, jammed together in the scanty space. She could scarcely lift the notebook high enough to read from it. Outside, Belle made faces at them, a remote but hilarious chaperone.

Fiona admired the decisive way he dictated his impressions of the scene they had just left. Then, in a changed tone, he added: "And hang on – I've got a quote. Exact words of Mrs P." He squeezed himself sideways so that Fiona could speak into the mouthpiece. "Slow and clear," he told her.

She read her notes as instructed. He pushed her

gently aside, spoke briefly to the person at the other end, and hung up. "Bless you," he said warmly. "It's a great help, having a good quote."

One way and another, she thought, it had been a wonderful evening.

CHAPTER
TEN

The first half-hour of the office day was often the most trying. Before settling down to his dictation Mr Bagshaw liked to scan his newspaper, reading bits aloud and making comments that infuriated Fiona, who dared not let herself utter a syllable in answer.

"A letter to the editor from Sir Almoth Wright! And it says he is a most eminent physician. He tells us that militancy is the result of mental illness. Fifty per cent of women go slightly crazy in middle age! He admits that some of the others have achieved distinction in various fields – by following male examples. But he says, 'in public life there are no good women, only women who have lived under the influence of good men'. Very true!"

Fiona could only swallow her indignation and console herself with the knowledge that any day now Mrs Pankhurst – admittedly middle-aged, but far from crazy – would be launching a new campaign that would set the country alight from Scotland to the south coast. There were suffragettes everywhere, local leaders in a dozen regions whose exploits were now legendary, like the irrepressible Edith Rigby in Lancashire, a friend of the Pankhursts and no less dedicated, constantly in and out of prison. When all these women swung into action Mr Bagshaw would really have something to exclaim over.

Meanwhile things were relatively quiet in London. Guy urged her to remember that there were other things in life besides the suffragette struggle. Rudd gave him press tickets for plays and concerts and art exhibitions, tickets that would otherwise be wasted. There were far too many events to cover in the paper.

Guy took her to the Old Vic, which had launched its first full season of constantly changing Shakespeare plays. Elsewhere they saw Mrs Patrick Campbell as the Cockney flower-girl in Bernard Shaw's *Pygmalion*, and the Russian ballet with Nijinsky performing his superhuman leaps. They went to a big concert to hear the first performance of Vaughan Williams's *A London Symphony* and to an art exhibition of the Post-Impressionist painters, whose flamboyant colours and odd perspectives were stirring such an argument.

Fiona had to agree. There *were* other things in life – fascinating things – besides the political fight.

When the warmer days came, said Guy, they would go walking in Epping Forest. "I'll look forward to that," she said, and meant it.

One evening, being at the theatre, they missed the news in the evening papers. It came as a shock when Mr Bagshaw greeted her exultantly in the office next morning.

"They've caught that woman again!"

She stared. "Mrs Pankhurst?" No need to ask.

She had appeared in Glasgow to start her new campaign. "They had her precious bodyguard massed on the platform behind her – these so-called 'ladies' had brought Indian clubs concealed beneath their skirts! They had hidden barbed wire amid the floral decorations along the front of the platform – " Mr Bagshaw spluttered with indignation. "But the police charged with their truncheons from the back of the hall – the women threw chairs at them and flowerpots, but it was in vain. At this moment," he concluded triumphantly, "Mrs Pankhurst will be in the train to London – and tonight she will be continuing her sentence in Holloway. They should never have let her out."

It was some time before he could calm his feelings enough to dictate his letters.

It was a great relief when she could escape from the office on some errand for him. Such an opportunity occurred the following day, and, as it was late in the morning, Mr Bagshaw told her to take her lunch-hour before coming back. Returning by way of Trafalgar Square she was delighted to encounter Guy. They agreed at once to have an inexpensive snack together in a teashop and, since she had ample time, to pay a brief visit to the National Gallery. "It's a free day," he said, "a chance not to be missed!"

He wanted to show her the famous Venus of Velázquez, recently bought for the nation after hanging for a century in a remote Yorkshire mansion, Rokeby Hall.

They climbed the great staircase and found it at once. The goddess was reclining on a grey-draped couch, the perfect foil for her pink flesh. She was studying her face in a mirror held by Cupid, so that it could be seen in reflection though she had her back to the viewer. "Ingenious," said Guy.

Two heavily-built men were sitting on a red plush seat, apparently indifferent to the master-piece. They showed more interest in the people pausing to admire it.

"Art-lovers?" queried Fiona ironically as she moved on.

"Policemen, more likely. Did you notice their *boots*?"

She laughed. "I know it's terribly valuable – but I don't see anyone snatching it in broad daylight!"

It looked enormously heavy in its massive frame with its thick glass covering. It was about six feet by four. A job for muscular removal men.

In the next room she saw a familiar face. Surely that was Mary Richardson? She had often seen her at meetings, once indeed talked to her. She was an interesting, attractive young woman. She had told Fiona of her Canadian childhood, how she had enjoyed riding the logs as they bumped and swirled their way down-river to the foaming rapids. Then, at fifteen, a few years in Paris – quite a change! A suffragette since 1906...

"Yes, I noticed her," Guy murmured as they passed on. "I wondered if she was really sketching – or just pretending to."

"She was too absorbed to recognize *me*."

They turned back towards the staircase. Twelve o'clock. One of the men stood up, murmured something about lunch to his companion, and departed. The other did not stir.

Mary Richardson was drawing near to the Velázquez masterpiece. There was something odd about the way she handled her sketchbook, a stiffness in her left arm. She moved from picture to picture, apparently aimless yet somehow purposeful. Fiona was seized with a sudden premonition that something dreadful was about to happen. She turned instinctively to Guy, a few yards behind her, studying a painting.

A sharp crack made her spin round again. The man had jumped to his feet, alert, and was gazing up at a skylight that a workman on a high ladder had been repairing only a few minutes before. His back was to the Velázquez – and to Mary Richardson, who was raising a small axe for a second blow.

Fiona gasped with horror. "Oh, *no*!"

Guy was at her side. "She's mad!"

The hush of the gallery changed to a tumult of shouts and hurrying footsteps. The drama was mixed with farce. A uniformed attendant, racing across the polished floor, slipped and sprawled headlong. Two German tourists hurled their guidebooks at Miss Richardson. She struck the picture several times, shattering the glass, before she was overpowered. The axe came skidding across the floor. Fiona saw that it was attached to a little chain of safety pins, by which Mary must have secured it inside her sleeve.

She started forward, but with no clear idea of what she intended. Guy seized her arm. "There's nothing you can do – nothing you *ought* to do – "

Mary had vanished into a scrum of struggling figures, from which she emerged handcuffed. There was a police inspector, his cap askew, demanding importantly: "Any more of you women in the gallery?"

The Canadian answered with cheerful contempt, "Oh, I expect so!"

"My God!" howled the inspector. He rushed off, bellowing, "Clear the gallery! Clear the gallery!"

They heard his voice echoing through the endless rooms, fainter and fainter. Within moments Fiona and Guy were being herded down the staircase with the other visitors and out into Trafalgar Square.

They had looked forward to their quiet lunch

together but they were fated to spend their time in hot argument.

Fiona flared up in defence of Mary Richardson. "But what good has she done?" Guy demanded. "And what harm? Not just to a world masterpiece, but the whole cause of votes for women? These outrages only turn the public against you. Smashing politicians' windows – and shop windows. Burning cricket pavilions, pouring acid on golf courses—"

"I don't like any of those things," she admitted unhappily, "but property seems to be the only thing the government cares about – the only way to strike at it!"

"You'll never win if you forfeit public sympathy."

"Sympathy doesn't seem much use. Scores of MPs say we have their 'sympathy'. When one of them brought in a private bill to give us the vote it passed its second reading with a three-to-one majority. And what happened then? The government blocked it. They can always block anything. Procedures, parliamentary timetables!" She almost spat the words in her indignation.

Mrs Pankhurst, she reminded him, had been fighting for twenty-five years, long before either she or Guy was born. Only latterly had she gone over to all this militancy. Out of utter despair.

Guy began to say that he *did* sympathize, but remembered how scornfully she had just spoken of sympathy. "Thank God I'm not a woman," he said with feeling.

She looked at him across the table and suddenly smiled. "Well, I thank God I am. In spite of everything."

As they walked along the Strand the newsboys were already selling the midday editions hot from Fleet Street. One headline ran :

SLASHER MARY –
Suffragette Slashes £45,000 Venus

Guy attended the court when Mary Richardson appeared before the magistrate. He got a bright-eyed welcome from Belle Isherwood when he squeezed in beside her in the crowded public seats.

"I've been away," she whispered. Her eyes opened wider when she heard that both he and Fiona had witnessed the scene in the National Gallery.

Caught in the act, Mary Richardson could hardly deny the charge. She pleaded justification. It had been a protest against Mrs Pankhurst's arrest in Glasgow.

She spoke with a calm dignity. "I tried to destroy this picture of the most beautiful woman in mythological history because the government is destroying Mrs Pankhurst – the most beautiful character in modern history! The nation is either dead or asleep. The government have closed all doors against us."

Her eloquent arguments did not save her from a

sentence of eighteen months hard labour. Guy tried to comfort Belle as they left the court. "The length of the sentence doesn't mean much. She'll obviously go straight on hunger-strike – she'll have a horrible few days until she's ill enough to be let out."

"And then there'll be this dreadful cat-and-mouse business – I don't think I could bear it, I'd never have the courage." In a lighter tone she asked: "Have you been to Lady Ottoline's again?"

"No." He hesitated.

"Oh, but you must! She liked you, she could do a lot for your career. If *I* go next Thursday, will *you*?"

He promised. She was right of course. He must think of his career. And he *had* made a determined start on his next novel. In case Lady Ottoline enquired.

"Fine!" said Belle. "I must fly – we've got people to luncheon." She waved down a taxi and dived into it. A girl, he thought, with a foot in both worlds. Elegant feet, too.

He also had a foot in two worlds. The grim world of the suffragettes, all idealism and anger – and the brighter world of laughter and vitality and colour, a constant stimulus to the mind and senses. He was torn between them.

It was a wild spring, and looked like being an even wilder summer.

CHAPTER
ELEVEN

Meanwhile Fiona, typing tedious documents for Mr Bagshaw, felt unbearably frustrated.

Mrs Pankhurst, released yet again, was struggling back to health, eager to resume the struggle if she could avoid rearrest. Her whereabouts were unknown. She flitted from place to place, repeating her first performance at Mouse Castle, her bodyguard obstructing the police while she vanished by some prearranged escape route.

Fiona relied for news on the movement's penny weekly. She was a volunteer seller and a distributor of leaflets, at any London gathering which she could get to after work. It was all she could do. Unlike some supporters of the cause she had no private means, no sympathetic husband or family. She dared not lose her job.

When plans were announced for the great demonstration outside Buckingham Palace she decided that she must be there, even though it would be on a Thursday, and in office hours. Mrs Pankhurst had written to the King, informing him respectfully but firmly that she would present herself at his palace gates on May 21st and ask that, as a loyal subject, she be given the chance to deliver the petition to him personally which his Prime Minister had refused to accept.

It would be *"absurd and futile"*, she wrote, *"for us to interview the very men ... who, in our eyes, have no standing in the matter, because we have not been consulted as to their election to Parliament. We have no power to vote for Members of Parliament, and therefore for us there is no House of Commons. But we have a King, and to him we make our appeal."*

It was vital that every possible supporter should be mustered for that afternoon. For the first time in all her working life Fiona invented a splitting headache and sought permission to leave early.

Mr Bagshaw was chivalrous. "Of course, of course, Miss Campbell! I see you have all the letters ready for me to sign. Run along, my dear, run along. I trust you will feel better in the morning." She thanked him, with secret guilt, and fled.

Belle was waiting, as arranged, in one of the Charing Cross Road bookshops. "Got your sash?" she asked.

Their sashes were better than banners on an occasion like this.

As they walked towards Piccadilly they discussed the recent House of Lords debate when a bill granting votes for women had been defeated by the government's large majority. "But Daddy voted in favour," said Belle. "I told him I'd strangle him if he didn't."

Both the Earl and Countess, she said, were sympathetic enough, though they did not approve of militant tactics. They had been horrified by Mary Richardson's attack on the Rokeby Venus. Luckily the damage to the painting had been much less serious than at first expected, and when the picture restorers had used all their skills it would be back on the wall – only better protected.

Belle's parents preferred the law-abiding policy of the National Union of Women's Suffrage Societies. "They tell me I'm young and impatient," she grumbled. "So I am! That other lot will never win us the vote."

As the Ritz Hotel loomed before them, she plucked at Fiona's sleeve. "Hang on," she muttered urgently. "I'd forgotten Mamma was lunching here today. They're just coming out. If she sees me she'll guess where I'm going."

They paused in the shady arcade, just short of the imposing entrance. A top-hatted hall porter was grandly beckoning a taxi. Fiona looked with interest at Belle's mother, a substantially-built lady wearing an immense hat piled high with artificial flowers and feathers.

"Would she forbid you?"

"She'd worry till I was safely home. And I'd hate that."

The Countess drove off. They turned into Green Park. On this sunny afternoon it was full of the usual strollers, but there were many others like themselves, making purposefully down the grass slope towards the palace, glimmering through the trees.

"Let's put on our sashes," said Belle. They unrolled them and slung them over their right shoulders, VOTES FOR WOMEN slanting across their chests.

The roadway in front of the high palace railings was solid with people. The straw hats showed how many men were mixed with the suffragette demonstrators. Overtopping them were the dark helmets of the policemen, and above them again the hundreds of mounted men, their horses' heads tossing.

"Just *look* at the police," gasped Fiona. "Hundreds!"

"She'll never get through," said Belle despairingly.

Fiona could only agree. Of late the police had been getting much tougher in their action. Years ago, veteran suffragettes had told her, it had been quite hard to get arrested. You could shout and wave banners to your heart's content, but the patient bobbies would do nothing. They would not arrest you unless you actually assaulted them. Some genteel ladies had found this extraordinarily difficult. They would drum feebly with their fists on the thickly uniformed chests of the

84

constables or stamp dainty feet on their massive boots without producing any reaction. The surest way to commit a technical assault was to spit in the officer's face, but some ladies were so inhibited by their strict upbringing that they could not muster the saliva to do so.

Those days were over. The police now had orders to be rough. Many disliked those orders intensely, but had to carry them out. In some, when sufficiently goaded, a hidden streak of brutality came to the fore. Fiona had heard tales of savage kicks and arm-twistings, of clothes torn off women's backs, faces deliberately scraped along rough walls and railings until they were covered with blood.

High above the palace roof the royal standard showed that the King was within. But what hope had Mrs Pankhurst of getting through to him – or even of reaching these outer gates – against such an overwhelming display of force?

Yet suddenly there was an outburst of shouting in front, the word spreading back through the crowd.

"She's there!"

"She's done it again!"

Somehow, miraculously, Mrs Pankhurst had appeared at the gates. Only afterwards did they learn how she had achieved it. She had spent the night at a supporter's house in Grosvenor Place at the rear of the palace. There she had made a brief speech to the other members of her deputation and the bodyguard. "Whatever happens, do not turn back!" She had started out at their head, but at some point slipped away, eluded the police and reached the gates alone before she was recognized.

Fiona heard, far in front, a woman's cry of dismay. "They've got her!" Then another woman's voice, firm and clear – was it the General's? "We mustn't let 'em! Come on!"

There was a surge forward. Belle went with it, shouting with the rest. Fiona plunged after her. The police had charged. She saw the bobbing helmets, the batons rising and falling. She heard screams.

Now came a clatter of hoofs. The mounted police were charging too, wielding long staves, not truncheons like the constables on foot.

The crowd thinned as people turned to escape. She got a clear view of Mrs Pankhurst. She was in the grip of an enormous police inspector with a waxed moustache and a chest lined with medal ribbons. He lifted her clean off the ground. She dangled in his hands, helpless as a doll.

Belle was rushing forward to help her, but a policeman on a grey horse shot between, blotting out all view of Mrs Pankhurst and the inspector. Fiona saw the rider change his staff to the hand holding the reins so that he could reach down with the freed one and clutch at Belle's sash. On the man's far side, hidden from view by his horse, a man was shouting an indignant protest. The policeman turned his head to swear at him.

"I don't care if you *are* 'press'! I'm arresting this young woman. If you obstruct me I'll arrest you too."

At all costs Belle mustn't get arrested. Fiona thrust her way through the mêlée. Belle was struggling, but the policeman's hold on her sash was relentless. The horse's hoofs scraped and drummed on the roadway as it turned this way and that. They were all now tightly enclosed by the crowd, shouting excitedly according to their sympathies.

Suddenly Belle's voice rang out, shrill with horror. "Oh, no! Not the poor horse!"

Fiona saw only a woman's upraised arm, a glint of sharp steel against that tossing head.

CHAPTER
TWELVE

Instinctively Fiona shut her eyes.

There was a harsh cry from the rider. The clatter of hoofs broke into a chaos of disordered noise. An unknown hand pushed her violently sideways and she went sprawling. Her eyes opened to a new view of the world from ground level, all blue-trousered legs and skirts and dancing hoofs.

The police horse was apparently unhurt but now literally uncontrollable, its reins severed. Over Fiona's head an elderly lady was saying with quiet satisfaction: "Secateurs! Nothing like them. In the garden – or anywhere else!"

With a swish of her long skirt the lady vanished into the crowd. No one tried to stop her. The policeman had dropped from the saddle and was striving to pacify his startled mount. He was too busy to arrest anyone.

Fiona struggled to her feet. Belle too must have fallen over, for she was being helped up by a good-looking young man in a straw hat, which had been knocked askew at a rakish angle.

"Guy!" cried Fiona with relief. "Where did *you* spring from?"

He grinned. "I didn't spring – I was shoved. Let's get out of here."

"But Mrs Pankhurst – " Belle gasped.

"They've driven her off in the Black Maria."

Belle allowed herself to be shepherded into the safety of St James's Park. Demonstrators were spattering the police with paint or pelting them with stones from holdalls they had brought with them. Others had equipped themselves with secateurs for cutting through the reins of the mounted men.

"It's all rather pointless now," said Guy.

"Pointless?" Belle echoed angrily.

"They've got most of the leaders. They'll be halfway to the cells by now. What do all these other women expect? To break into the palace – past all these police and then the guard? Chucking stones won't achieve anything."

"I'm afraid he's right," said Fiona.

"It's – it's so *defeatist*!" Belle's voice trembled.

Guy tried to calm her. "I think what we all need now is a cup of tea."

"Tea!" snorted Belle. Privately Fiona thought it a sound idea.

"Yes, tea." Guy studied them both with a quizzical expression. "I don't think I can take you into the Ritz – "

The girls became suddenly aware of their appearance. "Oh, dear!" said Belle, her sense of humour flooding back. "If I was at home in the country I could pretend I'd fallen down in the stable yard – "

"Mounted police do rather increase the hazards."

There was not much they could do beyond straightening their clothes and taking off their stained and tattered sashes. He escorted them to a secluded patch of shade near the teahouse and went off to fetch a tray.

"He is nice," Belle said, "though he makes me mad at times."

Fiona nodded. "I know."

"Men *can* be maddening, my brother especially. But there's something to be said for them – "

"You've found that?" asked Fiona gravely.

"Haven't *you*?"

Guy's return with a laden teatray provided an obvious answer.

He was on top of the world. He had sold an article – a really literary article – for five guineas. Five pounds *and* five shillings! He was in a mood to squander the shillings. Belle, in her present disreputable state, must go home by taxi. They picked one up in Trafalgar Square. Already the evening papers were out with startling headlines.

SUFFRAGETTES BATONED BY POLICE, cried the *Evening News*. SUFFRAGETTE RAID ON THE PALACE, retorted the *Westminster*, WILD SCENES.

The *Globe* shrieked: Armed Women Besiege the King!

In the taxi Belle asked: "Will you be at Lady Ottoline's tonight?"

He hesitated. "No, not tonight, I'm afraid."

"Too much excitement for one day?" She chuckled. "Next Thursday perhaps?"

"Will *you* be there?"

"If you are. I expect David Garnett will be, next week. His father could be awfully helpful when you – "

The taxi pulled up, as instructed, just short of her home. Guy paid it off. "I shall sneak in by the servants' entrance," said Belle. "They're so good, they always cover up for me."

Fiona could imagine that below stairs Lady Isabel was regarded as a household pet, universally loved. As the girl vanished down the area steps she turned to Guy, herself. "Thanks for the ride. I'll be all right from here." But he insisted, as she knew he would, on seeing her to Francis Street. But her urgent need of a bath and change of clothes made it impossible to ask him in.

"I trust you are feeling better, Miss Campbell?" said the old lawyer next morning.

"I'm quite recovered, thank you, Mr Bagshaw."

Yesterday's demonstration had made him more belligerent than ever. "What is the world coming to?" he demanded. "These dreadful women! Mr Asquith should really crack down on them."

91

Her mind flew back to that scene. The multitude packed dense around the great new memorial to Queen Victoria, the police charging, the batons gleaming in the sun... There had been plenty of "cracking down". She could not help saying: "Doesn't it seem odd, sir – everyone looks back on the old Queen as so wonderful, yet if she'd been anyone else they'd have said she wasn't even capable of voting?"

Mr Bagshaw bridled at this. "You forget what she owed to her husband's excellent guidance. The Prince Consort – "

So they were back to the pompous dictum of Sir Almoth Wright. No good women in public life, only women who had been influenced by good men. She could not let that pass. She said with deceptive meekness: "But Good Queen Bess never had a husband. Of course she did have a famous father – " She hesitated a moment, then with quiet satisfaction slipped in the dagger. "Henry the Eighth."

"We cannot spend the morning discussing history," said Mr Bagshaw shortly. "We must get on with the letters."

In fact, the government was now acting with the energy he demanded. Wholesale arrests – most of the leaders and many rank-and-file members – had been made during the Buckingham Palace disorders, which had gone on for several hours. Fiona realized with a shiver that only luck had saved Belle and herself from the same fate.

What would happen now? Presumably the quietly efficient Grace Roe had her orders from Christabel in Paris. Routine tasks such as the chalking of pavement slogans and the distribution of *The Suffragette* must go on. At midday on Saturday she went straight from the office to Kingsway to offer her services.

Grace Roe, as always, had a welcoming smile. Yes, it would be all hands to the pumps now. They were discussing what part-time help Fiona could provide, when heavy tramping feet were heard on the stairs. The room filled with blue uniforms. An inspector marched up to them.

"Miss Roe?"

"Yes?" She looked quite unruffled.

"I have a warrant for your arrest."

"Indeed? On what charge?"

"Conspiracy." He added the usual warning in official tones. The rest of the staff were being herded in from the other offices. He consulted a list in his hand. "I can see," he said with a smile, "that Mrs Drummond is not here."

"If she were, she would have spoken for herself by now!"

"I don't doubt it, madam." He surveyed the others, checking their names and functions – the office manager, the financial secretary, the assistant editor of *The Suffragette*, the sub-editor, the business manager. They were taken downstairs to the street. He turned to Fiona. Her heart gave a sickening lurch within her. "And who are *you*, young lady?"

"My name is Campbell. I—"

Grace Roe cut in swiftly. "This young lady is not a member of the staff. She is just a caller."

"Is that so? Well, her name's not on my list anyhow."

A sergeant stepped forward, holding out some foolscap sheets clipped together. "We've found this list of subscribers, sir —"

"Thank you. We'll go through this place with a toothcomb."

"I protest," said Grace Roe. "You have no right!"

"I have a search warrant, madam. If you will get your hat and handbag…" As she was taken downstairs after the others the inspector said to Fiona in a kindly voice: "If I may offer you a word of advice, young lady, I would say, don't get mixed up with these people. If you were a daughter of mine—"

"If you *were* my father," she burst out, "I shouldn't be proud of you for what you're doing!"

She went, and he made no move to stop her. Outside in the street the prisoners had been packed into a couple of taxis and were moving off in the direction of Bow Street. A constable had taken his stand outside the front door. Overhead she could hear the offices being ransacked. Helpless and despairing she could only walk away.

That evening the doorbell rang at Francis Street.

94

Daisy looked at her in alarm. They seldom had callers, especially late ones. Full of apprehension Fiona said: "I'll go."

Daisy said, with desperate optimism: "If it's your nice Mr Dangerfield you can ask him up. I'm here as a chaperone."

Heart in mouth Fiona ran downstairs. If it wasn't Guy it might at least be Belle.

It was neither. It was a shabby middle-aged woman she had never seen before, someone with a cockney voice.

"Miss Campbell?"

"Yes. Who is it?"

"I got this message for you. Confidential."

"Won't you come up?"

"Better not, dear. It's just this: 'The business has been transferred to 17 Tothill Street, Westminster.' Number seventeen, dear. Good night." The stranger walked away briskly towards the brighter lights of Tottenham Court Road.

CHAPTER
THIRTEEN

"Miss Campbell, is it?" The butler was respectful but cordial. "If you will hold the line, madam, I will ascertain if Lady Isabel is at home."

Soon a breathless Belle was speaking.

"I've got a lot to tell you," said Fiona. "Could you come out? A stroll in St James's Park perhaps?"

Belle laughed. "What could be more respectable for two gels on a fine Sunday morning! Quarter of an hour?"

"Fine. Corner of the square."

Walking down Tottenham Court Road, Fiona described yesterday's event at headquarters. "And then, last night, comes this mysterious woman with her mysterious message."

"Tothill Street is just near the Abbey."

"There may be no one there now – "

"I bet there will. If they sent you the address they must want you to make contact. You've not told

Guy? But, of course, he's not on the phone."

"And he's not a member."

"It's a pity we don't let men join," said Belle.

"I agree."

"I suppose he could join Miss Sylvia's lot."

Sylvia Pankhurst, more militant than her mother and sister, had parted company with them and now headed a separate organization in the East End, closely linked with Keir Hardie and the Socialist movement. She was even recruiting a "People's Army" prepared for a serious battle with the police. Men were more than welcome.

"I don't think Guy agrees with her views," said Fiona.

They crossed Horse Guards Parade. The leafy park, with its silver sheen of lake, stretched away to the distant façade of Buckingham Palace. They reached Tothill Street. The bare offices at number seventeen echoed with brisk voices. Some faces looked familiar, but the girls had to identify themselves and be checked on a list. "We have to be rather careful now," they were told.

Grace Roe had quietly prepared for yesterday's raid. Just as she herself had been secretly groomed to take Annie Kenney's place, so had she trained her own successor if she were arrested. No name was mentioned but already the office was beginning to function in its new premises.

Fiona was immediately set to work. Belle confessed with shame that she could not type, so was given envelopes to address, far too slowly, in the careful copperplate writing she had learnt at school. Then, apologetically, she had to rush off to luncheon. Fiona stayed the whole afternoon, sustained only on a cup of tea and an indigestible bun. Her offer to return next day, when she left Mr Bagshaw's, was warmly accepted.

Over the next weeks the pressure grew at Tothill Street. It was vital to keep up publication of *The Suffragette* as a sign that the movement was still very much alive. At least the authorities could not touch the editor. Safe in Paris, Christabel could still control it, though the difficulties of communication were multiplied.

To have banned the paper would have struck at the sacred British principle, the freedom of the press, and stirred up a hornets' nest in Parliament and throughout the country. The government took a more subtle line. If they could not stop the printing of the paper they could make it almost impossible to buy. A letter went to all wholesalers, asking them not to handle it. The big firms fell obediently into line and the retail newsagents were unable to get supplies.

To counter this the movement had to create its own system of distribution. There had always been volunteer sellers at meetings and demonstrations. That organization had to be vastly expanded. Somehow, by a miracle, *The Suffragette* never missed a week. Somehow it continued to reach the public.

Fiona and Belle plunged into this activity with

enthusiasm. Belle could take on daytime work, Fiona sacrificed evenings and weekends. Sadly she had to cancel a visit to the Old Vic with Guy, to see *Romeo and Juliet*, and a picnic he had planned in Epping Forest. She had greatly looked forward to both.

He did not take these cancellations well. He was already resentful because she could not tell him much about her work for the movement. She was vague even about the location of the new headquarters.

He challenged her crossly. "You don't trust me?"

"Of course I do. But we're not supposed to tell *anybody*."

"Am *I* 'anybody'?"

She hated to argue with him. "Of course not! But – you are a journalist—"

"Not that again! For heaven's sake—"

"I know you wouldn't pass on anything I told you in confidence. But suppose something leaked out from another source, and they thought it was from you, and they know we're friends, and—"

"Oh, never mind." At moments he sounded like a spoilt child. "So Sunday's off. And the Old Vic." His tone was a spark to her own smouldering resentment. She exclaimed furiously: "Do you think *I'm* not disappointed?"

He flinched at her anger and went quiet.

After two weeks at Tothill Street the police struck again. This time it was Belle who witnessed the raid. A positive army surrounded and invaded the premises – about eighty officers in all – and made a clean sweep of all the documents and files. Belle was returning from an errand to the post office. She found her way barred by a young constable who demanded her name.

His manner irritated her. She was not used to being spoken to like this. She never used her title in the office but retorted without thinking: "Lady Isabel Isherwood – if it's any business of yours!"

His manner changed. As he stammered apologies his sergeant intervened. "We need not trouble this young lady," he said sharply. To Belle he went on: "I beg pardon, Your Ladyship, I'm afraid this office is closed."

"Indeed?" She was prudent enough not to argue. She walked away. No sense in getting arrested. There had been a time when it had been the recognized way of winning publicity for the cause. Now the movement had enough martyrs. What it needed was people free to carry on the fight. Even so, she burned with indignation at the favouritism shown to her class.

Guy felt a similar anger when, a few days later, he went to the House of Commons to hear the Home Secretary speak on the subject of the hunger-strikes.

As a man, he got into the Strangers' Gallery without difficulty. Women, he noticed, were finding it harder. There had been cases, he knew, when they had interrupted debates with their shouting and unfurling of banners. Now the attendants were limiting the number of women admitted. And those who got in were all obvious "ladies" in speech and manner, well dressed, with expensive hats and gloves and handbags. Nobody of working-class appearance got past the doorkeeper.

An angry member was demanding that the government should leave the hunger-strikers to die. After one or two deaths in prison these fanatical females would learn how useless their policy was, and militancy would cease.

The Home Secretary did not agree. "For every woman who died," said Mr McKenna, "scores would come forward for the honour. They have a courage, part of their fanaticism, which undoubtedly stands at nothing. They would seek death. When there were twenty, thirty, forty – or more – deaths in prison, you would have violent reaction of public opinion." He looked grimly round the crowded benches. "I do not believe that is a policy which will ever recommend itself to British people. I am bound to say," he added emphatically, "that for myself I could *never* take a hand in carrying it out."

At least, thought Guy, this man has some principles.

When the uproar in the House subsided Mr McKenna went on to consider alternative suggestions. Should the suffragettes be deported to some distant island and marooned there? Their wealthy supporters would soon charter a yacht and rescue them. Could they be locked up in lunatic asylums? "I have on many occasions had them examined by doctors," he said. "In no case have the doctors been willing to certify them as lunatics."

Guy could have hugged himself. This would be a good quote to use in *The Suffragette*. He even wondered if Rudd would accept a satirical piece. But it was getting harder to sell Rudd anything on the suffrage theme.

It was now nearly mid-June. Police persecution and suffragette resistance were intensifying day by day. Afterwards, these weeks were to be remembered as "the midsummer madness". Fiona shuddered as she read the headline in the latest issue of *The Suffragette*. WOMEN DRUGGED AND TORTURED IN PRISON. Prisoners, struggling against the doctors and wardresses forcing food down their throats, were now being dosed with bromide to overcome their resistance. She wondered if she would ever have the courage to face such an ordeal.

The new headquarters were at the Brackenburys' house in Campden Hill Square. Mouse Castle was now the nerve centre of the campaign. For Fiona it meant a longer journey after the day's grind in Mr Bagshaw's office and another long journey home to her flat, though often she had Belle's company.

It was an inspiration to know the Brackenburys. Both daughters were well known as artists, Georgina for portraits and Marie for landscapes. Their father, General Brackenbury, must have been unusual for an army man, for his own paintings had won him election to the Royal Academy. For the past seven years the sisters had sacrificed their artistic careers for the suffragette cause, chairing mass meetings in Hyde Park and working devotedly in other ways. Two years ago they had served sentences in prison. So had their seventy-year-old mother.

With examples like that Fiona felt she could hardly complain herself if she crawled into her bed completely exhausted.

Mouse Castle was raided the day after Guy had listened to the Home Secretary's speech. It was now impossible to maintain an open headquarters. The organization went underground.

"I feel like a Russian revolutionary," said Belle cheerfully. "Chased by Cossacks and spied on by the Tsar's secret police! And this is England."

Somehow *The Suffragette* was still published and sold. But meetings had to be held secretly in private houses. Communications were made if possible by word of mouth, or, if written, conveyed in code.

One telegram Fiona had to dispatch somewhat perplexed the post office clerk. "Silk, thistle, pansy, duck, wool," he muttered, giving her a very odd look. "Is this right?"

"I do hope so," she said sweetly. "I *think* they are racing tips. I don't know what it means."

She knew very well. It was code for "Will you protest at Asquith's public meeting tomorrow evening, but don't get arrested unless success depends on it."

Friends – and enemies – were referred to by false names. Christabel Pankhurst became "Amy Richards". Other leaders were disguised as "Brer Rabbit", "Auntie Maggie" and "Clorf Ears". It *was* rather like being revolutionaries in St Petersburg.

July came. Mrs Pankhurst had won release again by determined hunger-strike – she was then rearrested, released as usual a few days later, and once more arrested as she was being taken to a meeting by ambulance. The government's relentless policy rallied more and more public sympathy for the cause. One July meeting raised nearly sixteen thousand pounds.

One evening Fiona and Belle were asked to carry out an errand on their way home. There was an urgent note for an address near Regent's Park. Would they, at the same time, deliver five dozen copies of *The Suffragette*?

The copies were packed in a small suitcase and a Gladstone bag. They set off with them in a velvety summer dusk, a light breeze off the park bringing a welcome freshness after the heat of the day.

After a while Belle lowered her voice. "Don't

look back. Take a glance when we cross the road. Two men – they were behind us ten minutes ago. They still are."

"Following us?"

"If they're not, it's an odd coincidence."

"Men do follow girls." Working in central London Fiona had learnt to deal with the problem.

"They don't look that sort. And they've made no effort to catch up with us."

They crossed the road. Glancing left and right, Fiona saw the men. After all the meetings and demonstrations she had attended in the past year she knew a plain-clothes policeman when she saw one. Belle was right.

"How maddening!" she whispered. "We must be getting near the house now. We're leading them straight to it! But we mustn't."

"After carrying these blessed bags all the way!"

"That can't be helped."

"But the note is urgent!" Belle had an inspiration. This area bordering Regent's Park was familiar to her from childhood walks with her nanny. "There's a little narrow cut-through between these houses – we used to race down and hide when we were small. We might somehow throw these men off the scent – "

"But how? They'll chase after us."

At that moment, by good luck, a possible solution offered itself. A uniformed constable emerged from a side turning and stopped under a street lamp, surveying the quiet scene. Without pausing to consult Fiona, Belle marched up to him and said in her grandest manner: "Officer!"

"Yes, miss. Can I help you?"

"Those two men. We're afraid they're following us."

He stared intently down the road. "Have they been annoying you, miss?"

"They haven't actually accosted us – yet."

"Well, I don't quite see what I can do, miss, if you're not lodging a complaint – "

"If you could just *speak* to them," Fiona suggested quickly. "Detain them long enough for us to walk on."

"We're almost home," said Belle – inventively but, as it proved, unwisely.

"Simplest thing, then, I'll see you safely to your door," said the constable helpfully, but greatly to Fiona's dismay. They were getting themselves into an awkward corner.

The two strangers were crossing the road, clearly intending to intrude upon the conversation. The constable began to say something in a discouraging tone, which changed suddenly into one much more respectful. "Sorry, sir! I didn't – "

Fiona saw the warrant card flash briefly in the lamplight. A gruff voice said, with the ring of authority, "That's all right. You may be useful."

"Sir!"

The stranger turned to Belle. "May I ask you to open that bag, miss?"

"Certainly not!"

106

"What have you got in it?"

"Only my night things. And so on," Belle added imaginatively.

"Open it, please."

"I shall do nothing of the kind." It was very much the Earl's daughter speaking. "If you think I am going to have somebody rummaging through my – my most intimate garments—"

"Then I'm afraid I must." He stooped, snicked open the suitcase, and revealed the neatly packed copies of *The Suffragette*. His colleague took the Gladstone bag from Fiona and revealed its similar contents. "I'm afraid," said the first man, "I must ask both you young ladies to accompany us to the station."

"Is it illegal to possess this paper?" Fiona demanded. But she was ignored. The man was concentrating on Belle. He was obviously determined to take them in for questioning. Any attempt at flight would be useless and would merely strengthen his suspicion. Things were beginning to look really bad.

There was only one useful thing she could do. Get rid of that urgent note, whatever it contained. She was sure to be searched when they reached the police station.

There was a handy grating in the gutter. She managed to draw the sealed envelope from her pocket and tear it into small pieces behind her back. Then, stooping forward suddenly, she dropped them between the bars into the drain. The other detective leapt forward but he was able only to catch a single scrap of paper before it vanished through the grating.

"Never mind," said his colleague. "Obstruction of a police officer. Perhaps conspiracy. Attempt to destroy evidence. Should do us very nicely."

CHAPTER FOURTEEN

At the police station Belle made no attempt to conceal her title. "Mamma will be frantic if she doesn't know what's happened to me," she explained to Fiona apologetically. "Perhaps," she said to the sergeant at the desk, "you will be kind enough to telephone my father and say where I am?"

"Certainly, my lady." There had been quite a stir of interest when she gave her name and address.

Fiona's mother had no telephone. It would be a terrible shock if a constable knocked on her door with the news at this late hour. Better to spare her that, and the ordeal of court attendance. She can be told soon enough, thought Fiona grimly, when we know the worst.

The charges were read out to them. Fiona had apparently kicked the detective's shin during that scuffle over the grating. He had suffered no serious injury, but it was enough to justify adding "assault" to the charges.

They would be taken before the Bow Street magistrate in the morning. "So tonight we stop here?" asked Fiona.

"That depends, miss. There's the question of bail."

"I don't want bail." Suffragettes usually refused bail on principle. It meant promises of good behaviour, obedience to a law they regarded as unjust. In earlier days strangers had often tried to go bail for them, out of sympathy or to save the government from bad publicity. One of their fiercest opponents, Winston Churchill, had even offered to pay fines for them, but they had refused his help.

Belle took her cue from Fiona. "I don't want bail either."

A few minutes later her father marched into the charge-room. Fetched out of some important function, he looked very distinguished, thought Fiona, in his white tie and tails and glittering decorations. The policemen practically sprang to attention.

He kissed Belle. "What *have* you been up to, my dear? Your mother's no end upset. Never mind, soon get you out of this—"

"I don't want bail, Daddy!"

"Beg pardon, my lord," said the sergeant helpfully. "She's given her age as only nineteen."

"That's right."

"So it's not for her to say. You being her father – "

"That's all right, then."

"Daddy!"

The Earl ignored her wail of protest. He looked at Fiona – a friendly look, she thought, not as disapproving as she might have expected. "This your friend?"

"Yes, this is Fiona. Fiona Campbell."

"Howdy-do, Miss Campbell! Can I be of any help to *you*?"

"Certainly not over bail, thank you, my lord. And I have no father, so I can make my own decision." She smiled, not wishing to sound ungrateful. "My overnight accommodation seems to be arranged for me!" There was an answering twinkle in his eye.

The formalities took a few minutes. Belle whispered, "I'm so sorry – it's humiliating, having to leave you like this."

"Never mind. As I used to say to my friends after school, 'See you tomorrow!'"

A policeman called a cab for the Earl. Fiona was led away to a cell.

So it had happened, she reflected grimly, the thing she had always secretly dreaded. She lay on the hard plank bed, reviewing the full implications. She had often wondered, with gnawing fear, if she would have the strength of will to face those implications. The first step – to refuse bail – had been easy enough. But to refuse food... She was already famished after the long day. She had been looking forward to a late-night supper at Francis Street. She would be offered nothing here until breakfast tomorrow morning. Would she be able to refuse it then?

Dawn came, the pitilessly early dawn of high summer, and after further endless hours of waiting, the key turned in the lock and they brought her a mug of tea, a slab of brown bread, a nub of butter. She could not resist temptation. She gulped down the tea. She was not going to attempt a thirst-strike anyhow. Only the most dedicated did that. She had heard horrific stories of the effects of dehydration. She would only refuse food – after this final breakfast. She tried to satisfy her conscience with the thought that she would need all her strength to face the magistrate.

Belle would certainly be having a good meal. She imagined her at Bedford Square, tucking into eggs and bacon, lifting the silver dish-covers on the sideboard in quest of kedgeree or devilled kidneys. Poor Belle! In the end this ordeal would hit her twice as hard. With her delicate upbringing how would she stand it?

Unless, of course, the Earl somehow contrived – but no, the time had passed for pulling strings in high places. The government was ruthless. Too many society women were tainted with suffragette sympathies. People like Lady Constance Lytton. It had not helped her that she had been the Earl of Lytton's sister. Now, after several hunger-strikes and forcible feeding, she was likely to be an invalid for life.

The room beneath the court was crowded – there were half a dozen of last night's drunks, still looking much the worse for wear, and two young girls whom her mother would certainly have described as no better than they should be. There were policemen and solicitors. It was easy to spot Belle.

Belle waved and beckoned, introducing her to the man she was talking to. "This is Mr Glover. Daddy insisted on my having a solicitor. If you care to accept Mr Glover's assistance, Daddy will be very pleased—"

"That's very kind of him. But I think I must speak for myself."

"Just as you please." Mr Glover looked relieved.

When they were taken up the stairs into the dock Fiona saw the Earl at once, and then – what was more of a surprise – two rows behind him, a pale-faced Guy who met her look with a weak and worried smile.

The girls both pleaded not guilty. The detectives gave their evidence. It sounded well rehearsed. The stipendiary magistrate, a red-faced little man, questioned Fiona.

"These – er, magazines. Where were you taking them?"

"It was an errand for a friend, Your Worship."

"But to what address precisely?"

"I did not know." There was a little stir in the court. The magistrate frowned.

"Then presumably, Lady Isabel, you knew?"

"I'm afraid not." A greater stir. The man's jaw dropped.

"You both ask me to believe that you were carrying these bags through the streets – yet neither of you knew where you were taking them?"

"If I may explain, your worship," said Fiona politely, "you asked us for the 'precise' address. I had been told the name of the road but not the number. Lady Isabel knew only the number. She was not to tell me that until I told her we had reached the road."

"And what was the purpose of this tom-foolery?"

"If we had been stopped and questioned earlier neither of us could have given away the full address."

"Ha! That seems strong evidence of a conspiracy!"

Mr Glover popped up. "By your leave, Your Worship – I appear for Lady Isabel Isherwood – if I may raise a point?"

"By all means, Mr Glover."

"Conspiracy implies an agreement to commit an illegal act – "

"Certainly!"

"This weekly paper, *The Suffragette*, whatever we may think of its contents, is not illegal. There is nothing illegal in buying it or in possessing a number of copies. I submit respectfully, Your

Worship, that my client could not therefore be guilty of conspiracy."

"I will consider your submission, Mr Glover. Now, to continue…"

There was something highly suspicious in the two young ladies' continued refusal to give the address they were making for. Their suffragette connection was obvious and many suffragette activities *were* illegal. Lady Isabel had lied about the contents of the bag she was carrying. At the very least they had obstructed the two detectives in their enquiries. The prisoner Campbell had obstructed them further by the deliberate destruction of a letter she was carrying, in the course of which she had assaulted the officer who was attempting to restrain her.

Summing up, the stipendiary said he had formed the opinion that Campbell, though only slightly the elder, was the prime mover in this affair. "Women like you," he declared, "are the cause of the present breakdown in law and order. They must not be surprised if their continuing defiance brings increasingly heavy sentences. You will go to prison for three months. With hard labour."

Surveying Belle with a more-in-sorrow-than-in-anger expression, he went on: "It is particularly painful for me to pass sentence on a young person like yourself, of gentle upbringing, from a well-known – I may indeed say a noble – family, famous in the annals of this country. By your folly – and no doubt through the bad influence of unsuitable companions – you have brought disgrace upon that family and in particular your parents."

Fiona looked at the Earl. His expression was one of contempt, but not (she felt certain) for his daughter or even for herself. He was shaking his head in disagreement.

The magistrate droned on to the end. "So I fear that you too must go to prison – you leave me no alternative. For two months."

"With hard labour?" Belle reminded him. In her resolve to have no favouritism she was almost pert.

The man scowled, suddenly hostile. "I was about to say so," he said sharply. "Take them down!"

Turning at the stairs Fiona caught a last glimpse of Guy's face. He looked devastated.

CHAPTER FIFTEEN

It was a short drive to Holloway in the horse-drawn Black Maria. They talked in undertones. It was good to be with Belle again. "We're in this together," said Belle.

Unfortunately they were not – for long. After the cheerless formalities of admission and the changing into uniform – a coarse dress and apron marked with the government broad arrow, a cap tied with strings – they were marched off to separate cells.

Fiona's was number twenty-two. A round yellow badge with that number hung on a nail inside. "You pin that on your dress," said the hard-faced wardress. She was not merely *in* twenty-two, Fiona realized, she *was* Twenty-two. She had no name now, no identity.

The door clanged shut. She was alone. She looked round. A plank bed tilted back against the wall. Folded bedding. A stool, a table, a tiny basin for washing, a bar of coarse yellow soap.

The midday meal was brought. Brown bread, potatoes, cabbage. "You can take it away," she said. "I'm on hunger-strike."

"You'll soon change your mind." The wardress left the food.

Fiona had not long to wait before grasping the significance of that remark. The women in the nearby cells must have been in prison for several days. Some, being suffragettes on hunger-strike, had now reached the point of forcible feeding and the full horror of the procedure was all too audible. The cell doors concerned were left wide open while it was going on, so that it was not lost on anyone within earshot.

It would begin with cries of defiance, changing quickly to an outburst of terrible screaming, going on and on. Then agonized coughing and choking, renewed screams, more choking, until at last the noise subsided into a fearful, exhausted moaning.

In the end Fiona had to stop her ears. It seemed callous, cowardly. But it was unbearable. Would *she* be able to stand this? Somehow, God help her, she must.

The interminable day went by. Supper came – more brown bread, butter and milk. She drank the milk. How long had she to keep this up? Four – five days? Could she endure that long?

She tried to occupy her mind. At school they had learnt poetry and recited. She had been good at it. Her memory was stocked with poems she had never forgotten. She called to mind old favourites. For brief periods she could push back the prison walls.

She thought of her mother and her sister. They must have been told by now. She longed for the chance to explain, to comfort them. But at this stage neither letters nor visits were allowed.

She slept fitfully. Then distant bells rang, keys rattled, iron doors crashed. She had a quick wash in cold water, with that gritty soap. Her own door was flung open. "Empty your slops, Twenty-two!" Breakfast. It took an effort to ignore even the dry brown bread. She drank from the pint mug of watery gruel, then stopped. It would rank as "nourishment".

The hard labour was hemming sheets. Her labour card showed that she must do at least fifteen a week, hemmed top and bottom. She had loved sewing as a little girl, sitting companionably with her mother by the fire. This was rather different.

At half past eight she was let out to line up with the others and march into chapel. She saw Belle and whispered, "How are you?" Belle smiled back. "Bearing up—" A wardress snarled, "Stop talking, Thirty-three!" They could not sit together. The chaplain said prayers and they sang hymns. It was good to use one's voice again.

At exercise one had to walk up and down the yard in silence. At intervals she came face to face with Belle and it was just possible to exchange some sort of greeting, silently mouthed and lip-read by the other. But they were closely watched and shouted at if this was observed.

Her first ravenous hunger had passed. It took less will-power to reject food. The lack of nourishment was beginning to take its toll.

Even with the wardresses no conversation was allowed. One seemed more human than the rest. When Fiona refused her dinner she whispered: "Won't you eat a little, miss? This starving won't achieve anything." Fiona shook her head. "I hate to see you like this," said the woman as she went out.

There were times when Fiona's head swam, when her hand trembled as she drew the needle through the sheet. At exercise she stumbled. On the third day she looked in vain for Belle. She broke the rules and asked the friendly wardress: "Is Miss Isherwood – Number Thirty-three – all right?"

"She's a bit better – "

"Could you give her my love?"

The wardress shrank back in alarm. "Sorry, miss – much as my job's worth! Carrying messages between prisoners!" She made a hasty exit. The heavy door crashed shut.

Belle was in chapel next day. She gave Fiona a pallid smile. The effects of the hunger-strike were beginning to show.

Fiona herself had a visit from the prison doctor.

He took her pulse and checked her heart. "How long have you been refusing food? Four days? You must stop this foolishness. You *must* take some nourishment." She shook her head. "Then I've no alternative. I shall have to feed you."

She shrugged her shoulders. He went out. She had given up any attempt at work, she could no longer keep her stitches straight. She was not taken out to exercise.

So, the time had come – nearly. Perhaps it would not be as ghastly as it always sounded. Hundreds of other women had endured it. She too would survive.

Now came those brisk footsteps in the corridor, halting some distance away. The usual screams began, then the choking, the vomiting... Poor Belle! Would *she* be going through this? The appalling sounds came nearer. Fiona's heart beat wildly, almost stopped when the doctor strode in, followed by the wardresses carrying the equipment.

"Ah," he said crudely, "another young turkey for stuffing!"

She glared at him venomously as two women gripped her arms and stretched her out on her bed. Another, the sympathetic one, moved behind her to hold her head, and a fourth seized her ankles. Others held a funnel attached to an enormously long tube, and jugs to pour into it.

The doctor stooped over her. "I must put a gag in your mouth to keep it open. The wooden

121

one is less painful. But if you compel me to use the steel one – "

She clenched her teeth. One must resist. One did not co-operate with these monsters. So in the end it was the steel gag that was rammed into her mouth and pressed down painfully into her gums, forcing her jaws unnaturally wide. She closed her eyes as they began to push the thick rubber tube down, down, endlessly down her throat.

She was choking. She struggled spasmodically. Her knees shot up. The woman gripping her ankles pulled them down again. She tried to lift her head, but could not. They were pouring the meat juice down into her resisting body. The overwhelming impulse to vomit gave her momentarily super-human strength to break their vice-like grip upon her. Then the horror started all over again.

At last the doctor said crossly, "That must do for now." He glared down at her, dabbing himself with angry disgust. "If you are not going to be rea-sonable," he warned her, "I shall feed you through the nose next time." The women trooped out after him, carrying their hideous paraphernalia. She lay exhausted, soaked and stained by her own vomit.

"Next time," he had said. "Dear God," she moaned. But the movement's motto was *No surrender*. She must hold out.

CHAPTER SIXTEEN

After the last glimpse of Fiona's dark head vanishing below the rail of the dock, Guy pushed his way out into the glaring sunshine of Bow Street, dazed and disorientated.

He had often worried about the risks the girls were taking. Sooner or later, he had told himself... He had never realized it would hit him as hard as this.

What could he do? Ten minutes later he found himself mechanically climbing the stairs to his room. His typewriter stood waiting reproachfully. He must lose himself in work, the time-honoured remedy. But the scene in the courtroom persisted in his mind, blotting out all thought of his novel.

What *could* he do? He ate some bread and cheese, then walked down to Fleet Street. Perhaps he could persuade Rudd to print something that would at least relieve this awful blockage of frustrated feeling.

Rudd was not helpful. "Our readers must be getting sick of the suffragettes," he said. "You mustn't get into a rut, lad. Look around. There's more to life than votes for women."

It was hard to argue with Rudd. He was repeating Guy's own advice to Fiona, to broaden her interests.

"There's the Irish question." Rudd puffed a cloud of tobacco smoke fiercely across his desk. "We may wake up any morning and find a civil war's broken out there. Or the Balkans – that murder of the Austrian archduke at Sarajevo the other day. That could start a war too. But we're getting into the holiday season – people want to read about Charlie Chaplin or the new flying machines. And there's sport."

"Yes," said Guy with sarcasm. "There's always sport."

Back in Lamb's Conduit Street he managed to write a few pages of his novel, only to tear them up. They did not live. There was only one thing he wanted – passionately – to write. A letter to Fiona. But she would not be allowed to receive it.

That evening he walked up the dreary Holloway Road until he reached the prison. Somewhere behind those blank twenty-foot walls the girls were enduring God knew what. The gates were as blank as the walls. There was a bell, but prisons were not like hospitals where you could enquire for friends within. A more practical idea occurred to him.

He could not believe that Belle's parents were in similar ignorance of their daughter's welfare. Surely the Earl would have ways of getting news. Tomorrow, Guy decided, he could at least ring *his* bell. He slept better that night, and after breakfast he hurried to Bedford Square.

"I am sorry, sir," said the butler. "His lordship has just gone out."

"Would it be possible to see the Countess?"

The butler eyed him cautiously. "You are not a journalist?"

Guy avoided the question. "I am a friend of Lady Isabel's." He handed the butler his card.

"If you will step inside, sir, I will enquire."

In a couple of minutes he was back, relieved Guy of his hat, and ushered him into a small room where Belle's mother sat at a desk strewn with letters and crested envelopes. Guy apologized for the interruption.

She smiled rather wanly. "A welcome interruption! Look at all these letters. Like condolences after a death in the family. You're a friend of Belle's?"

"We met at Lady Ottoline Morrell's." Unnecessary to say that they had met previously at a suffragette rally.

"Of course!" cried the Countess. She fingered Guy's card. "Mr Dangerfield! The clever young man who has written a novel. Belle has spoken of you."

"I wondered if you had any fresh news of her?"

The smile faded. "She's not allowed letters. But my husband has managed to ascertain that both the girls are … as well as can be expected."

"I was going to ask. Miss Campbell's a friend of mine too."

"My husband was *most* impressed by her behaviour in court." She looked at him gravely. "You will understand, we are greatly upset by this affair. It is quite dreadful to think of what they must be going through. But we are with them – all the way. The logic of their cause is unanswerable. It is wicked that things should come to this. I blame Mr Asquith. But I would, wouldn't I?" She smiled again. "*We*, of course, are Conservatives."

He knew he must not take up any more of her time. He stood up. "If we get any more news," she promised, "I will send you word. I see you live not far away." She offered her hand. "Go along then, Mr Dangerfield, and write some more of your witty novels. We need something, God knows, to make us laugh."

Writing witty novels was the last thing of which he felt capable. Remembering Rudd's advice to keep abreast of the world's other news, he decided to pay another visit to the House of Commons. The Prime Minister was that day going to move the Irish Amending Bill in a desperate effort to avert the impending violence in that country. The Strangers' Gallery was crowded.

Guy was not destined, however, to become any wiser about the Irish question. There was a buzz of

126

surprise from the MPs below when Mr Asquith rose and announced that its discussion must be postponed.

"We meet today," he went on solemnly, "under conditions of gravity which are almost unparalleled. The issues of peace and war are hanging in the balance."

A man behind Guy whispered impatiently: "We know that. The Irish—"

Another voice answered, "It's not that. He means we're on the brink of a *European* war!"

And so it seemed, unbelievably, as Guy began to catch up with the news he had scarcely taken in since the girls' imprisonment.

He had heard that Austria, infuriated by the assassination of its archduke, had sent the Serbs an ultimatum. But how could it possibly affect Britain? Over the next day or two, as one sensational news item followed another, he began to see.

The Tsar of Russia, traditionally the protector of his fellow Slavs, the Serbs, was mobilizing his immense armies to fight his rival, the Emperor of Austria. But Austria's natural ally was the third great European emperor, the Kaiser of Germany. By the end of the week the London papers were headlining a German declaration of war on Russia.

The situation was getting ugly. France was Russia's ally. She would have to back her against the Germans. Britain was nobody's ally. She was not legally bound to enter the quarrel. But she had a close tie of friendship with France – and, said some, could she *afford* to risk the French being beaten, and Germany left the most powerful country in Europe? That Saturday the British were arguing such questions anxiously.

Guy did not alter his own plans for Sunday. It was the day he and Fiona had meant to take their long-postponed walk in Epping Forest. It was sad to go alone, but better than moping in his stuffy room. He would be thinking of her wherever he was. Better to do so in the cool shade of the beeches and promise himself that next time she would be walking at his side.

That day, though, the woods rang with the laughter of the East End crowds, and he found his own loneliness unbearable. By the evening, leg-weary and sunburnt, he felt he must have company. One of the Fleet Street pubs offered an obvious solution.

It was full of newspaper men, all hotly discussing Winston Churchill. Was the fellow mad? He'd often been thought unsound. What he had done now was really the limit.

Yesterday, as First Lord of the Admiralty, he had urged the cabinet to mobilize the fleet. France might be at war with Germany at any moment. The German fleet could then sail into the Channel and bombard the French coast. This, Churchill had said, must be prevented at all costs. Asquith and the others had rejected his proposal.

Today, incredibly, without consulting them again – without even a word to the King –

Churchill had taken it upon himself to mobilize the Navy. Had he gone out of his mind?

"Or have the rest of 'em?" demanded one veteran journalist. "We may thank God for Winston yet!"

Sure enough, next day, August Bank Holiday, the cabinet hurriedly approved Churchill's action. Germany *had* declared war on France – but her warships had not tried to pass through the Dover straits. Instead, the Kaiser had sent Belgium an ultimatum, demanding the right to march across her neutral territory and attack the French frontier.

It was the Belgian King's defiance that really stirred the sympathy of the British public. They hated a bully like the Kaiser. They would go to the help of "gallant little Belgium".

One by one, day by day, the nations of Europe seemed to be toppling like ninepins, knocking over their neighbours as they went. The fatal telegrams were flickering between the capitals, proclamations being signed. Millions of Russian peasants were being called up from the harvest fields and sent marching in their drab uniforms, endless columns of them, along the dusty roads towards the frontiers. In Belgium the uhlans, the dreaded German lancers, were galloping across the Belgian fields. Even here in Britain the summer manoeuvres were broken off on Salisbury Plain so that the War Office could prepare for real hostilities. And the ships of the Royal Navy were steaming to take up their secret stations.

It was the strangest Bank Holiday Monday. By nightfall Guy was one of a vast multitude outside Buckingham Palace, singing *God Save the King* and clamouring for the monarch to appear on the balcony. There was the usual know-all in the crowd around him. He was reassuring everybody. "Mark my words, if it does come to a war, it'll be all over by Christmas!"

What a difference, Guy thought, from that afternoon on this same spot when he had rushed to save the girls from the hoofs of the police horses! He wondered what they would be thinking at this moment – if they had any knowledge of what was going on in the world outside...

CHAPTER SEVENTEEN

I feel like death, I must look like death, Fiona reflected gloomily. But evidently the doctor considered she could stand another day or two of this torture.

This was the fourth day. Each visit from that team of disciplined monsters was like a recurrent nightmare. She was paying the price for starting as a healthy young woman with no heart weakness or other disability. These fiends would only stop the treatment if they got scared that she might die on their hands. Perhaps, though she struggled against the gag and that vile tube, and seemed to bring up all those nourishing fluids they poured into her, she might be keeping down more than she realized? In that case the ordeal might go on for ever. That thought was intolerable. She groaned, turned her head on the rough pillow, and closed her eyes.

What was that hubbub in the distance? Oh,

no, not yet! It couldn't be time. But far down the corridor there were the successive crashes of opening doors flung back on their hinges. That was the devilish cunning of the procedure. When several prisoners were forcibly fed their cells stood open throughout, so that the cries could be heard by the others.

There was no screaming today. Just shouting. For a wild moment she wondered if it meant mutiny – or a rescue attempt from outside. It could not possibly succeed. She was so weak, she could not lift a finger to help. She got up off the bed and stood up unsteadily, clutching the table for support.

The key turned, her door swung back. It was the wardress she still thought of as the kind one.

"Can you walk, dear? You're going out."

"Out?" Fiona swayed. The strong hand held her.

"I'll help you. I'll fetch you your own clothes."

"But – what –"

"It's the war. All you suffragettes are going out. Your leaders have called the campaign off. We must all stand together against the Germans."

Waiting in the doorway Fiona made what sense she could of the excited voices calling from cell to cell. Was that Grace Roe? She had not heard that voice since the day of the head-quarters raid. It sounded different now. Only later did she learn that Grace Roe had been subjected to forcible feeding three hundred times and her throat was painfully inflamed. But hoarse and weak though it was, the firm instructions could only have come from that indomitable organizer.

"Listen, everybody! No one's to sign any undertaking. Promise nothing! Everything must be negotiated by the leadership."

The wardresses gave up their half-hearted efforts to collect signatures. Fiona's hand was too shaky to hold a pen.

Suddenly Belle was at her elbow. They hugged each other till they almost fell over in the corridor. "I've got my handbag back," Belle cried. "I can pay for a cab – if we can get one. You must come home with me."

"But what will your parents think?"

They soon got the answer to that. There was a welcoming crowd outside the gates. There, in the midst of the banners, the purple, white and green ties and sashes, stood the man she had seen in court, with a lady who must be the Countess. And talking to her was the other man she had seen in court. Guy.

Belle's mother took charge. "You can't possibly go to your flat alone, Miss Campbell. You need nursing. So does Belle. I'm a mother – two are much easier to nurse than one! We have the motor waiting. Mr Dangerfield, you will come back with us for luncheon? Though goodness knows what these poor girls can be allowed to eat! Our doctor will advise us. Then I shall pack them both off to bed."

"Isn't it lovely to be *free*?" said Belle wickedly. "Not to be ordered about all the time!"

POSTSCRIPT

More than three years later, in one of her countless letters to Guy, Fiona was able to write:

January 11th, 1918

Now at last I can tell you we've won the vote! After FIFTY YEARS' struggle! As I told you before Christmas, the bill had passed the Commons – and today's Daily Mirror *says it has gone through the Lords with a two-to-one majority. Now we only need the King's assent, and that's automatic. So we were right to suspend our campaign and put all our energies into the war effort. Even the Bishop of London said he was "wholly converted" to the cause – women will be so essential to world reconstruction after the war. Belle's father made a splendid speech as well. I'm glad that Belle (who sends her love!) persuaded me to join her in the*

Land Army – I was lucky to get to the same farm. She's wonderful with the horses. I'm not, but I'm useful at tidying up after them! I'm better with that old motorbike – and I haven't fallen off again – yet. How wonderful that you saw the Turks surrender Jerusalem to General Allenby! I'm thankful you're out there, not in France. I pray every night that you'll come safely home..."

And he did.

SONG FOR A TATTERED FLAG

Geoffrey Trease

The time is December 1989.
The place, Romania.
The event, revolution!

The last leg of his school orchestra's concert tour brings eighteen-year-old Greg Byrne to Bucharest, Romania – his mother's homeland – where he hopes to make contact with a distant cousin, Nadia. But the city, as Greg quickly discovers, is a dangerous, fearful place, held in the iron grip of dictator Nicolae Ceausescu and his dreaded Securitate. What Greg cannot know, though, is that he and Nadia are about to be involved in one of the greatest events of modern history!

"Ingenious plotting... Vivid."
The Times Educational Supplement

CALABRIAN QUEST

Geoffrey Trease

Her heart nearly stopped... The figure was human – but the head upturned to meet her incredulous stare was the head of a wolf.

A fifth-century Roman christening spoon is the catalyst for this thrilling adventure which sees Max, a young American, travel to Italy with Andy, Karen and her cousin Julie on a quest for lost treasure. It's not long, though, before they encounter some sinister happenings and find themselves in conflict with the local Mafia...

"A gripping story of archaeological adventure... The tale rattles along, demonstrating an unputdownability as durable as [Geoffrey Trease] himself."
Mary Hoffman, The Sunday Telegraph

"From storytelling such as this, readers are infected with a love of books."
Jill Paton Walsh
The Times Educational Supplement

SHADOW UNDER THE SEA

Geoffrey Trease

A hand grabbed the collar of her denim jacket and jerked her savagely to her feet. She found herself looking down the barrel of Shulgin's gun...

In the new Russia of glasnost and perestroika, making friends can be surprisingly easy – as Kate discovers when she meets Stepan and Marina. But the bad old days aren't over yet – not while the sinister Comrade Shulgin is alive and plotting...

"Crime and archaeological discovery and teenage romance are deftly interwoven in this beautifully paced, engrossing story."
The Times Educational Supplement

THE FLITHER PICKERS

Theresa Tomlinson

"Northern sea, silver sea,
Bring my daddy home to me,
Hush the waves and still the sea,
And bring my daddy back to me."

Life is hard for the fisher folk living and working on the north-east coast at the turn of the century. The men face death daily in the often stormy sea, while the women, the flither pickers, gather bait from the shore. Children who are too young to work, like Liza Welford, are supposed to go to school. But what have books and sums to do with a child of the sea?

Based on real events, this novel is illustrated with black and white photographs of the period by the celebrated Frank Meadow Sutcliffe.

"A gritty, touching novel of the North Yorkshire coast." *The Guardian*

THE ROPE CARRIER

Theresa Tomlinson

"This little lass is strong. She will carry the ropes, and walk for ever."

Set in the late eighteenth century and illustrated with contemporary engravings, this is the story of Minnie Dakin, the youngest of the ropemaker's daughters. The life she leads, underground in a huge cave in Derbyshire, is hard but not unhappy. But when she's called to Sheffield to join her ailing sister, Minnie finds a harsh world of poverty, squalor and injustice, which tests her courage and strength to the full.

"Theresa [Tomlinson] has blended all of the historical detail into her story with striking compassion… An impressive companion to *The Flither Pickers.*"
Books for Keeps

KISS THE KREMLIN GOODBYE

Alison Leonard

"He didn't put his arms round her straight away, but he leaned and kissed her over the space between them...

The Drama Club trip to Moscow takes a thrilling and complicated turn for Megan, when she meets the engaging Kostya, one of the stars of the Student Theatre...

Set at the time of the opening of the Berlin Wall, this is an absorbing story about young people of different cultures coming together – in friendship, fury, desire and understanding.

"Funny and moving... wholly convincing."
School Librarian

MORE WALKER PAPERBACKS

For You to Enjoy

☐ 0-7445-2304-4   *Calabrian Quest*
                  by Geoffrey Trease   £2.99

☐ 0-7445-3082-2   *Song for a Tattered Flag*
                  by Geoffrey Trease   £2.99

☐ 0-7445-1450-9   *Shadow Under the Sea*
                  by Geoffrey Trease   £2.99

☐ 0-7445-2043-6   *The Flither Pickers*
                  by Theresa Tomlinson   £3.99

☐ 0-7445-3604-9   *The Rope Carrier*
                  by Theresa Tomlinson   £3.99

☐ 0-7445-2360-5   *Kiss the Kremlin Goodbye*
                  by Alison Leonard   £2.99

☐ 0-7445-3098-9   *Wolfsong*
                  by Enid Richemont   £2.99

☐ 0-7445-1466-5   *Backtrack*
                  by Peter Hunt   £3.99

**Walker Paperbacks are available from most booksellers,
or by post from B.B.C.S., P.O. Box 941, Hull, North Humberside HU1 3YQ**

24 hour telephone credit card line 01482 224626

To order, send: Title, author, ISBN number and price for each book ordered,
your full name and address, cheque or postal order payable to BBCS for the total amount and
allow the following for postage and packing:

UK and BFPO: £1.00 for the first book, and 50p for each additional book to a maximum of £3.50.

Overseas and Eire: £2.00 for the first book, £1.00 for the second and 50p for each additional book.

Prices and availability are subject to change without notice.

Name _____

Address _____

_____